FIRES IN THE DARKNESS

NORA ASH

ABOUT THE AUTHOR

Nora Ash writes thrilling romance and sexy paranormal fantasy.

Visit her website to learn more about her upcoming books.

WWW.NORA-ASH.COM

ONE

LIGHTNING

For once, Lightning remained under the duvet when his conscience snapped back from the heavy shroud of sleep, eyes closed against the pale sunlight filtering in through the windows. His limbs were heavy with the kind of exhaustion only phenomenal sex could inflict upon his preternatural body. Really, *really* phenomenal sex.

Despite his relaxed state, his lips pulled up in a smile at the thought. It didn't even matter that he'd had to share the experience with his least favorite person in the entire universe—fucking Kathryn blew his mind so thoroughly that the sight of The Shade balls-deep in her only made him want her more.

Soulmate.

Yeah, he wasn't fooling anyone. It wasn't just fucking Kathryn that blew his mind. It was everything about her.

Lightning heaved a deep sigh as his thoughts turned decidedly mushy. The drugged-out sensation from last night's sex took the edge off his usual fear that followed any exploration of Mirome's word for her. The one starting with "soul" and ending in babies and happily ever after.

Ah, and *there* was the rush of anxiety. Great.

How the hell was he going to survive the intense ache in the core of his soul for everything a—a *wife* had to offer, when he knew better than most that there was no peace to be found in St. Anthony? Especially not for someone foolish enough to love another. Trust another.

The sex-haze melted away, leaving gloomy depression in its wake. Lightning groaned. Since when did he allow himself to angst all the fucking time?

Since Kathryn.

He snorted at his mind's immediate response. No wonder Bright wanted her so bad, seeing as she seemingly had the power to royally scramble two of the city's strongest supes' brains.

Screw it. If he was going to spend this much time fretting about the girl, the least he could get was a good morning fuck first. It was pretty damn hard to be depressed while pounding into Kathryn's wet little snatch.

His cock was in firm agreement and already at full mast when he rolled over to persuade the blonde woman to spread her thighs for him again, perhaps by burying his tongue between her lower lips. Only, his arm, when he stretched it out to wrap her into his grasp, didn't meet soft, pliable flesh.

Lightning froze as his palm skimmed over solid muscle.

"Keep your paws to yourself, or you're losing a hand," a deep, decidedly male voice grunted.

Lightning cracked his eyelids, already knowing what he'd see. Sure enough, The Shade stared grumpily back at him, still with the remnants of sleep veiling his glowing eyes.

Which was probably the only reason the villain hadn't made good on his threat yet.

Lightning removed his hand from The Shade's chest and scowled back at him. Not exactly who he'd hoped to roll over and see first thing. And why wasn't he more freaked out that he'd fallen asleep next to his enemy? The Shade could have unmasked him in his sleep. Even killed him. And here he was, only mildly annoyed that he couldn't ease the tension in his cock. "Where's Kathryn?"

"Dunno," The Shade grunted, stretching his bulging body. Apparently, the villain didn't have any quarrels about having been asleep and vulnerable next to his enemy, either. "Probably in the bathroom. Kitten?" The last bit he shouted in the direction of the closed bathroom door.

Silence met them as they both listened for any movement behind the only internal door in the apartment.

Lightning frowned and sat up, straining his hearing until his preternatural abilities kicked in—the ones that would let him hear her heartbeat clear across a crowded room, if necessary.

"Son of a bitch!"

The Shade's outburst underlined the complete lack of any sign of life, save their own and the muted sounds from the lower levels of the building. Kathryn was gone.

His enemy was up and out of the bed in the blink of an eye, pulling on his pants.

Lightning mirrored him, his heart pounding. If Bright had somehow managed to sneak in while they'd been asleep and kidnap Kathryn again, it should be possible to catch any lingering remnants of the distinct, sharp scent all supes shared. But all he picked up was his own and The Shade's, mixed with Kathryn's sweet essence. The whole apartment reeked of sex and stale sweat.

"Where the fuck has she gone? And why is it so goddamn hard for her to just stay put?"

It wasn't until he heard The Shade's frustrated growl that it dawned on him that Kathryn had walked out of there of her own will.

That girl was going to be the death of him.

"Maybe we fucked a few too many of her braincells loose last night," Lightning said, as an unpleasant mix of worry and hot anger welled up in his chest.

"How did she even sneak out of here without us noticing?" The Shade rubbed the back of his neck and sent Lightning a glance that perfectly reflected his own feelings: concern for her safety, anger at her idiocy, and just a sliver of uncertainty at how he'd allowed himself to rest so completely in his enemy's presence that she'd been able to leave without alerting his otherwise impeccable senses.

Lightning shrugged. He didn't know, and he didn't feel like dwelling on it right now. He'd much rather try to figure out where the fuck she'd gone off to so he could go get her back. And then perhaps teach her what happened to unruly soulmates who insisted on sneaking out and putting themselves in danger. Thoroughly and repeatedly.

The Shade snarled, "Oh, for fuck's sake!"

Lightning spun around. The Shade was crumpling a note in his hand, and Lightning's heart dropped to the pit of his stomach as a strange sense of déjà vu set in. Had Bright somehow snuck in? If he had her... if he hurt her...

"The little idiot's gone off to meet her friend. They got some big-shot reporter involved, but *oh*—she's conveniently not said anything about *where* they're meeting him. Why is she so *incredibly* stubborn? And she really expects us to just hang around and wait for her to traipse back home 'sometime before lunch'? I swear, when I get my hands on her..."

The frustration in his voice made Lightning's heart crawl back up in his chest where it belonged. As annoying and plain stupid as it was of Kathryn to go out on her own, at least she hadn't been kidnapped—again. He rolled his shoulders to ease some of the tension wreaking havoc on his muscles. Before Kathryn, he'd never entertained the idea of having a masseuse on speed dial. Damn her.

"Who's the reporter? Maybe we can track her down if we pop in and search his home. There might be a wife or a girlfriend who knows where he went, or at least a diary with his appointments."

The Shade scoffed and tossed the paper back on the desk where he'd found it. "Oh, I'm sure you'd love working with him. It's Nick Coleman—almost as big of a fucking saint as you. But before you get any great ideas, may I remind you that involving humans in this is just going to end up getting them killed."

It was curious, really. Where his heart had dropped to the bottom of Lightning's stomach before, this time, it stayed put. Only instead of beating steadily behind his ribs, it skipped several beats as ice-cold realization froze him to the spot.

Oh, no. Oh, powers above, no. If Kathryn thought she was meeting Nick Coleman, then she was walking into a trap for sure.

The instrumental part to a metal song penetrated through the sudden silence, making him jerk and whip his head around in search of the source of music.

The Shade reached into a hidden pocket in his pants and produced a fancy-looking cell phone.

"Now's not the time to be taking phone calls," Lightning snapped. "And really, 'Testament'? Way to be a fucking stereotype."

The Shade ignored him and frowned at his phone's display. "It's Kathryn."

"Kathryn's got your *number?*" Lightning asked in disbelief. "What the fuck, were you planning on taking her to dinner and a movie too?"

The Shade sent him an admonishing glare before he pressed the button and lifted the phone to his ear. "Miss Smith?"

Miss Smith? Awfully formal for someone who'd just spent the night banging the girl's brains out.

Lightning narrowed his eyes as the truth hit him with astonishing clarity. The Shade had found her in his human disguise—and that right there was his regular phone. But then the question was: why the hell was Kathryn calling a regular human while out on her investigative adventures?

"*...They can do that, with their pheromon—*"

The muffled voice on the other end of the phone sounded like it came from far away, as if the speaker wasn't holding it up to their face, but the voice belonged to Kathryn without a doubt.

A sharp smack interrupted her.

"*Shut. Up! You don't get to speak about him like that! He loves me, and I love him. Not all of us are too thick to form real relationships. Just because no one will ever really love you doesn't mean you get to disparage my relationship. He and I are one—and you are nothing, like you always were! Do you know why I'm the only one who still keeps in touch with you? It's because I pity you! No one else could be bothered, because you're so pathetic, Kat. You always were and you always will be. And it's your own damn fault you're going to die. If you hadn't dropped your panties for the first supe who showed you any sort of interest, Bright wouldn't care one whit about you."*

Lightning bared his teeth in a silent snarl. The other speaker sounded a whole lot like Kathryn's pushy friend— the one she was supposedly off talking to Nick Coleman with. The second he'd heard that name he knew something was terribly wrong, and from the sound of this conversation, he'd been right.

"You are the pathetic one!" The sudden fierceness to Kathryn's voice surprised him, but also made a flame of pride flicker in his chest, despite his intense worry. His Kittykat had claws. *"And you're a fake, a liar, and now an accomplice to murder. Well done, Trish. I hope you'll remember this moment when you realize that you are nothing more than a toy to him. And you! They trusted you! You were their teacher. Their friend! That's the only thing they agree on. How can you betray them like this?"*

Time seemed to pause as he and The Shade looked at each other across the room. There was only one person she could be speaking to like that, but... it made no sense. The complete shock and denial in The Shade's gaze mirrored his own feelings. No. There was absolutely no way—

"I am not betraying my old students, little dimwit. I am merely ensuring that I don't get on Bright's bad side. And if they'd had any sense, they would have heeded my warning and done the same. It's either be on his side, or perish, and I have no intention of ending my existence for the sake of opposing a man who simply wants what is our race's

*birthright. You humans—you are so inferior that you will
never grasp it. Why should we live in the shadows? Cower at
the thought of angering lesser beings than ourselves?*

"*I am not too surprised that Lightning is trying to be
noble and 'save humankind'. Saddened, but not surprised. But
that The Shade has chosen to follow him in his ridiculous hero
complex? That is an unexpected loss—and one I will hold you
fully responsible for, you worthless cunt.*"

"Mirome." The Shade breathed his name, too low to
disturb the conversation on the other end of the call, but the
betrayal came through loud and clear.

Lightning set his mouth in a grim line and met his
enemy's gaze. Now was not the time to deal with the monu-
mental loss echoing through both of them. Mirome had been
their teacher, their only father figure for most of their lives,
but right now, he had their soulmate in his possession. If they
wanted any chance at getting her back, they would need to
stay focused. Mourning would have to wait.

The Shade worked his jaw, but his darkened eyes stayed
focused as he nodded. He was on board.

Somewhere behind the turmoil of painful emotions
ripping him apart from the inside, Lightning had the errant
thought that they worked surprisingly well together when it
came to Kathryn.

"*W-what do you mean?*" Kathryn's voice had lost its
sharp note, her fear coming through the woolen connection
loud and clear. Lightning fisted his hand at the thought of
her scared face as she faced the man who had betrayed
them all.

"*As if you didn't already know. You are their mate—their
'soulmate,' as you humans so poetically call it, and neither
would ever allow you to be unhappy. Your ridiculous attempt*

to expose Bright has brought them down with you, and they don't even care that they are slaves to a simple, human cunt. And that, my dear, is why I am going to personally kill you, once Bright has used you to lure them into his trap."

A loud crack was followed by a pained grunt and the unmistakable thud of a body falling to the ground.

Footsteps sounded next to phone, then the splintering sound of someone teleporting, followed by more static and more footsteps. A slamming sound, as if someone closed a heavy metal door, but no more voices.

The Shade disconnected the call and looked at Lightning with a grim determination that almost blocked out the pain behind his eyes. "Ready to kill our race's Secret Keeper and Bright's human plaything? Or do you have any heroic feelings of mercy you think will get in the way of my revenge? Because I'm telling you right now—if you do, you need to stay out of my way."

Lightning returned his stare. "I assume you have an auto-tracer on that phone."

"Of course I do."

"Then what are we waiting for?"

TWO

KATHRYN

My head pounded from blinding pain once the darkness finally faded. I squinted up against the flickering light from a fluorescent tube and took in my surroundings. I was inside a small room made entirely from concrete, with only the single strip light and a heavy metal door to break up the monotony.

Good thing I didn't suffer from claustrophobia. I touched my head lightly where the throbbing originated from, and winced. *Ow!* Being knocked out hurt a hell of a lot more than what movies suggested.

When I pulled my fingers back, a bit of red streaked them. Mirome clearly hadn't held back.

My stomach roiled at the sight, and I had to swallow several times to settle it. The deep breathing also helped clear my head just enough that I could fully comprehend my shitty situation.

I'd been kidnapped—*again.* And the girl I'd thought was my best friend had betrayed me so profoundly I couldn't even fully wrap my mind around it, what with my brain throbbing with pain so intense it made my eyes water. My only consolation was that there at least was a chance that I'd alerted The Shade to my situation. Not that there was any guarantee he'd picked up, but maybe it'd have gone to voice mail and recorded enough of what happened to make them realize that Mirome had betrayed them. And intended to use me as bait.

Hopefully, he and Lightning would work out a way to get me out of this mess, because I was all out of ideas.

Just then, I spotted my purse lying on the floor by the wall, and my pulse sped up. My phone! Maybe they hadn't taken the time to remove it, and I'd be able to call The Shade again.

As swiftly as my aching skull would allow, I crawled over to it and shoved my hand inside to rummage for my lifeline. When my palm connected with the familiar shape of my cell phone, I nearly cried from relief.

A relief that quickly died. As soon as I pulled my phone out, it became obvious why they hadn't bothered to go through my stuff before leaving me in here. The concrete walls were blocking off the reception, leaving my phone as little more than a fancy paperweight.

So much for not being a helpless damsel. I sank down against the wall and rested my head in my hands as the small burst of hope fizzled away. Not only did I keep getting freaking *kidnapped*, but my attempts at helping just seemed to make everything worse.

I don't know how long I sat there, wallowing in self-pity, but it seemed like hours. When the door to my holding cell finally opened, my throat was dry from thirst and my joints stiff from sitting in the same position for so long.

"Get up."

I looked up to see Trish standing in the doorway, aiming

a gun at me. If I hadn't been numb from emotional overload, it would undoubtedly have rocked me to my core to see someone I used to trust so completely pointing a weapon at me. As it was, I only felt a wave of disgust at how low she'd turned out to be.

"What, or you're going to shoot me? Wouldn't your beloved Bright be pissed if you killed me before he's used me as bait?"

"It's not like you don't have plenty of body mass I can shoot at without killing you. I doubt he'd mind if I blew your kneecap. Now *get. Up.*"

I obeyed slowly, steadying myself against the wall when my head began to spin and the pain from my wound intensified. Trish motioned for me to walk outside so I did, grimacing as each step made my head throb. There wasn't anything left to say, and no reason to plead with her to spare me. She was too far under Bright's thrall, and apparently quite happy to be there.

Trish guided me down concrete hallways lit up by sparse strobe lights that made me think we were in some sort of a bunker. The notion wasn't dispelled when the narrow hallway opened up into a room a few times bigger than the one I'd been kept in. There was a sturdy chair bolted to the ground in the center, with equally sturdy straps attached to the arms and legs, and a metal grid underneath it. On the near wall hung a row of wicked instruments that looked like they belonged in a slaughterhouse. Mirome stood next to the chair, caressing one of the armrests with a thin smile.

"Ah, there you are. Come, sit. We have a little chatting to do before Bright gets here."

My steps faltered as I took in the scene, my eyes flicking

from the terrifying tools on the wall to the grid underneath the chair. It was a torture chamber.

I don't know how the seriousness of the situation had managed to elude me up until then, but even after I woke up in a concrete cell with a splitting headache, some part of me had expected The Shade and Lightning to sweep in and save me before anything really awful could happen. Just like they'd done every time before.

"No, no... you can't!" I was vaguely aware I was babbling as I backed against the barrel of the gun Trish was holding. I froze, and she jabbed it hard against my spine.

"Stop being such a fucking coward," she snarled. "Sit down, or I'll shoot you and you'll still get put in that chair."

Every hair on my body stood on end when a sharp, metallic click announced that Trish had cocked the gun, but I was physically incapable of getting any nearer to the chair. My muscles had stopped responding to my brain's commands, even as it was screaming for me to do something, anything.

I didn't get a chance to unfreeze as Mirome evaporated with a *snap* and a purple cloud of dust, only to reappear next to me in the same second. He grabbed me by the shoulder and threw me into the chair. I landed with a painful *thump* and yelped from the impact, but before I could as much as scramble to get up again, he'd secured my wrists and ankles tightly to the chair.

"There. That's much better, isn't it? Neater." He sent me that sickly smile of his, but behind the mask, his eyes were cold as ice. "Now, as I said... let's have a little chat. Bright will be so thankful if I poke a few holes in you and see if any delicious secrets spill out."

"I don't have any secrets!" I spat, cringing back in the

chair when he casually strolled toward the wall with the tools. "Bright already asked me everything when he captured me the first time. You're wasting your time."

"Ah." Mirome pulled out a long, pointed piece of metal with an elaborate handle, almost like a miniature rapier. It looked like the work of a craftsman. A sick craftsman. "But I won't find it a waste of time. I find torture... quite relaxing. So even if you don't tell me anything of interest, I guess I can just write it off as recreational pastime, hmm?"

I did my best to control my breathing as he picked a knife off the rack as well and turned around, but I couldn't look away from the sick look of glee in his eyes. "Now, are you ready to sing, little bird?"

<hr />

"WELL WELL, you're a stubborn thing, aren't you? Or perhaps you truly are just clueless."

I didn't have the energy to answer Mirome's taunting, nor the desire to. It had taken everything I had to not plead and beg for what felt like the past many hours, but was likely much less. Time had a way of standing still when someone had you tied up while inflicting the worst kind of pain on you.

I breathed heavily and sagged in the chair, trying to get my shaking body under some form of control. Everywhere hurt, from the long gashes all over my skin to my fingernails, which had suffered the torment of the long, needle-like tool. When Mirome wiped blood off the knife in front of me and studied it carefully for any damage, the sight of it made my stomach churn until I had to lean over as much as my binds would let me to spit up bile.

"So dramatic," he said as he gave the long needle a similar level of scrutiny. "We didn't even get to play with any of the electric tools, and here you are, retching all over my floor like a real drama queen. But perhaps we can resume this later, once Bright's had his fill of you, hmm? You may not know Lightning's true identity, or even where he keeps his base, but let's be honest here—I don't much care. I just like to see you writhe in agony, you worthless piece of human trash. I want you to beg for forgiveness for taking my boys away from me before I kill you. What do you say, want to make a little bet on how long that'll take?"

I had never hated anyone as much as I hated this man— my torturer, the one who had betrayed the men I loved. That hatred gave me enough strength to lift my head and spit in his face. "Go to hell, you psychopath!"

Mirome put the needle aside, carefully and with measured precision, before he wiped his cheek of my spit. With equally controlled movements, he bent down in front of me with a hand on each armrest and looked me straight in the eyes, a thin smile on his lips. "You are going to regret that, girl. I promise you."

The seething hatred in his icy stare matched my own, and I felt my resolve wither under his gaze. He was crazy— stark, raving mad—and I knew he would make good on his promise to break me before he killed me.

"Please." The plea bubbled out of my throat without conscious thought, spurred on by the desperate instinct to fight for my life. "Don't."

Mirome's mouth pulled up into a smirk. "See, that's much better. You just practice—" His voice faltered and his gaze shot toward the hallway Trish had brought me down. Then his face contorted with frustration and he straightened back up, cursing low before he spun around to face the only entrance to the room.

"What's happening?" Trish, who had remained quiet during my torture, scrambled up from the floor behind me and came into view. "Is someone coming? Is it Bright?"

Mirome didn't answer, but from the tension in his body, it was obvious that he wasn't expecting whoever he'd heard. When my human ears finally picked up a muted thud from further down the hall, like the sound of a door being closed, my heart sped up. If it wasn't Bright, then maybe...

"Kathryn!" The sound of my name rung through the concrete room before my eyes even picked up that we were no longer alone. Two more supes had joined us, one dressed in midnight black, the other in charcoal and crimson. Lightning and The Shade.

My entire body shuddered with relief so strong tears welled in my eyes—but in the next moment, Mirome was behind me, pressing the knife against my throat.

"Don't do anything rash now, boys," he said as the blade bit into my skin, causing fresh pain to shoot through my already abused nerves.

I bit back a whimper and looked at the two masked men standing just a few yards away, fists clenched and teeth bared. Their eyes were firmly fixed on Mirome and the knife, but the rage in both their gazes was palpable, even from my vantage point.

"*Rash?* You kidnap our mate, *torture* her, and now hide behind her like a coward. You are going to die, *teacher,*" The Shade spat. "How painlessly depends on you. Lower the knife and we'll make it quick."

"Well," Lightning said, the murderous intent as clear in his voice as it was on his face, "quick*er.*"

"You've got to see it from my side," Mirome said. From the change in pressure of the blade against my throat, I could tell he was shifting ever so slightly behind me. "Bright gave me a choice—go with him, or die. And I plan on living for many, many more years."

"There was always the option of not betraying us," The Shade growled. "But I don't give a shit about your reasons—I just want to sink my blades into your gut and see your entrails spill out. You *will* die for this."

The room exploded in noise and streaks of color as my supes attacked. Mirome spun out of the way just as The Shade's sword cut through the air above me. Then everything turned into a blur, their movements much too fast for my eyes to keep track of. Only the sounds of fighting, punctuated by angry hisses and metal screeching against metal, came through the whirl of preternatural bodies locked in combat, until suddenly, I saw Trish running for the exit.

But my former friend never made it out of the torture chamber. Suddenly, she stopped, as if someone had yanked a string attached to her body, and looked down in shock. I hadn't seen the weapon that penetrated her chest, but I saw the blood blooming out to color her clothes. Then she fell to the ground in a boneless heap. Dead.

I should possibly have felt something. Remorse for how our long friendship ended, pity for how lost in Bright's games she'd become. But I felt nothing as I stared at her crumpled form, apart from the pain in my own body from the torture she had witnessed in silent acceptance.

As abruptly as the fighting started, it stopped. The three supes paused as if on cue, stilling long enough for me to make out their individual figures. Mirome had long, red-rimmed gashes slashed through his elaborate costume and a bloody lip. He was hunched by the door, breathing heavily. Both Lightning and The Shade had cuts of their own, undoubtedly from Mirome's knife, but neither looked to be in as bad a shape as their old teacher.

The pause in the fight only lasted a few seconds, but it was too long. Mirome straightened from his hunched position and gave them a mock-salute. Then the air blurred, and he was out the room. The sound of a door being flung open echoed through the hallways and into the torture chamber a split second later.

"*Fuck!*" The Shade whacked the wall with one of his swords, making sparks fly from the impact. "Fuck, we *had* him!"

"It doesn't matter." Despite Lightning's words, his tone was dark. He wiped a trickle of blood from the corner of his mouth and turned back around to me. With a gentle touch he knelt down next to the chair and loosened my bindings, being careful not to aggravate any of my wounds.

"Right," The Shade muttered. "Can we move her?"

"I think so." Lightning brushed my hair away from my face, checking me over for any unseen injuries. "Think you can handle being carried, Kittykat?"

I wasn't about to stay in this hellhole any longer than I had to. I carefully flexed my hands and winched as the movement made my wounds bleed anew, but no longer being restricted was blissful. "I-I think I need to go to the hospital."

THREE

KATHRYN

When I finally opened my eyes after the unpleasant after-shock of teleportation had eased, I realized that the two supes hadn't taken me to a hospital. Instead, we were at the top of what looked to be one of the highest skyscrapers in the city, with the wind howling around us from all sides.

"I really do need a doctor," I croaked. "I know we have to defeat Bright, but I'm... I'm not doing too good." Unwanted images of Mirome's sick smile as he pressed the needle up underneath my fingernails made me close my eyes and breathe deeply until they passed. Somehow, I doubted I would ever be the same person as I had been before I'd experienced true evil.

"No. We'll take care of you, Kitten." The Shade closed his hands over my shoulders, deftly avoiding any cuts or stab wounds. "It will be faster."

I wanted to ask what he meant, but I didn't get a chance before he and Lightning had easily maneuvered me down on the roof in a seated position, their bodies shielding me from the harsh winds.

"This kind of magic is not something we do often. It will take a lot of concentration. Please do your best to be still during so we can take your pain away." Lightning brushed a gloveless hand gently against my bruised cheek. There was anguish in his glowing blue eyes, and a rage only barely contained by his iron will.

I nodded, a little dazed by the intensity of his gaze. Then he nodded at The Shade, who was holding me from behind, and closed his eyes.

All the tension, all the emotion drained off his face as he sat in the howling wind with my hands in his. For a moment I thought he was simply meditating, until a gentle heat started to emanate from his hands into mine. Seconds later, a similar warmth penetrated my ripped shirt and seeped into my sides where The Shade was holding me. The heat traveled slowly, millimeter by millimeter, right into my bones. And in its wake the throbbing in my flesh seemed to ease, until there was just a dull ache left.

When Lightning finally opened his eyes again, it had been nearly an hour, and what was visible of his face was soaked with sweat.

"I'm afraid that's as much as we can do," The Shade rumbled from behind me. "Neither one of us are natural healers."

I stared in wonder at my arms. What were once bleeding gashes were now fresh, pink scars. "I had no idea you could do that." It came out as a broken whisper. And then came the tears.

Both men held me so wonderfully close while I finally got to cry all the fear and pain out, letting me break down in their shared embrace. Whispered words of comfort blended into my wails and the wind, until finally, after what felt like an eternity of sorrow, I was done.

I sagged between them, grateful to be wrapped up in their steely arms with their strong bodies surrounding me in a perfect shelter against the world. I felt empty, but also calmer than I had in a very long time. This was my home—this was where I belonged, where I'd always belonged. With the two men who would come for me no matter what, no matter where—and no matter how badly I fucked up.

"I swear to all that is holy, if you *ever* take off on us like that again, I'm personally going to make sure you won't be able to walk when I'm through with you."

I blinked in shock at Lightning's angry growl against my shoulder.

"He's right," The Shade echoed from my other side. "Consider this your very last chance at being allowed any sort of personal freedom. If you get yourself kidnapped one more fucking time, I'm done playing nice with you. Don't push your luck again."

My mouth dropped open at the injustice, outrage dampening my otherwise warm and fuzzy thoughts. So much for the sweet moment of peace in their arms. "Are you serious? I just got betrayed by my best friend, and kidnapped by *your* old teacher! How the heck was I supposed to have known that would happen? You certainly didn't!"

"Neither of us get kidnapped every other day, now, do we? You're too weak to run around town on your own, investigating whatever clue you think has popped up. From now on, you're running *everything* by us before you as much as think about acting, or you *will* end up on lock-down. I'm sure The Shade has more than one holding cell across town. Got it?" Lightning pulled back enough so he could look me in the eyes, though he didn't release his hold on me.

A blessed rush of anger heated me up from the inside, making me set my jaw and glare back up at the superhuman in front of me, though my death-stare was meant for both of them. "Sure, I got it. You're as controlling and mean as apparently every other supe in this Godforsaken city. Perhaps it's all part of that special DNA that makes you shoot laser beams from your eyeballs and fart fairy dust—all that *awesome* has to come with a few drawbacks, right? But you want a human plaything to boss around, you got it! Just give me a dose of supercharged pheromones and I'm sure I'll happily comply with your every whim. Want a blowjob while we're at it?"

To my chagrin, Lightning's eyes lit up with amusement at my rant. "Well, if you're offering—" he began, the smirk already forming on his lips. Thankfully, The Shade interrupted before I lost complete control over my rapidly flaring temper.

"It's not a control thing, Kitten. It's that we can't fucking live without you, all right?" He grabbed me by the shoulders and spun me around so he could look at my face. "I heard what Mirome told you about us—about what you are to us. I can't lose you. Neither of us can. And if you keep putting yourself in danger, we have no choice but to keep you safe, forcibly. You understand?"

I didn't. Not really, anyway. I hadn't forgotten about the word Mirome had used—*soulmate*—but it wasn't like I'd had any sort of time to reflect more on it since, what with having been busy being kidnapped and tortured. How could them choosing to mark me with their magic make us soul-anything? But when I looked into his eyes, dark with emotion, I knew that whatever my complicated feelings for him were, they were reciprocated, at least to some degree. I didn't know if it was the same for Lightning, but the gentle ghost of his lips over the back of my head confirmed that he certainly felt *something*. Even if he was extraordinarily bad at expressing it.

"We'll talk more later, when all this is behind us." Lightning's voice was low, but he was standing so close to me, pressed against my back, that I could hear both the words and his oddly vulnerable tone perfectly over the wind. "But until then, please, Kathryn, please don't put yourself at risk again."

Well, when he phrased it like that... I nodded and swallowed the lump in my throat. "Okay. Okay, I can do that, but no more sidelining me. I know I'm not as strong as a superhuman, but clearly, my reporter instincts are an asset. I was right about Mirome, and you refused to even listen. If you want me to stay put, you need to not shut me down like that again."

The Shade sighed, the way his lips pinched indicating that he wasn't entirely thrilled about the compromise, but he nodded nonetheless. "All right. You got yourself a deal."

Lightning grunted behind me, and I chose to take it as confirmation that he was on board, too.

"Okay, well... thank you. Speaking of my reporter instincts... if Mirome wanted me for Bright, and we assume that the mayor did visit him like the servant said, maybe the mayor should be our next stop? I know you say it's complicated to kidnap a politician of his level, but I think he's our best bet."

"I agree," Lightning sighed. "After today, it's past time to be cautious of political infringements. Which also means

that we should visit the other council members and find out
if they, too, are in Bright's pocket, or if we can rely on them to
help us."

"Let's start with Whisper," the Shade said. "After Bright,
she has always commanded the most respect." He stepped
back a bit and grabbed my hand, spinning me halfway
around so Lightning could grab the other. "On three."

THE PLACE we teleported to was a dark, Victorian-style
house set in an overgrown garden on the outskirts of town.
Once my now familiar bout of motion sickness settled, I
frowned up at the windows. "This doesn't look very Secret
Lair."

"It's not. It's her Meetings House—most Council
Members and a few other supes have one, to allow for visi-
tors," Lightning said. "But Whisper spends a lot of her time
here. She's usually the one we go to, if we have any issues we
don't particularly want to debate at a meeting. Like a sheriff,
if you will."

"We shouldn't bring Kathryn in. For all we know,
Whisper might be on Bright's side too," The Shade said. He
flattened his lips in a frown.

"I'm not leaving her on her own," Lightning continued,
giving voice to the dismay on both supes' faces.

I sighed. "Really? You can share me in bed and trust
each other enough to fall asleep after, but you still think the
other's going to take off with me?"

Lightning grimaced, probably at the reminder of having
been naked and vulnerable through an entire night in The
Shade's presence. "She's got a point. Fine, I'll go, but I'm

sure I don't need to say what will happen if you do take her?"

The Shade rolled his eyes. "You have my word that I won't hide her from you until Bright's been eliminated."

Lightning shot him a dark glare. Then his eyes flicked to mine and the glare softened. Without another word, he turned around and walked at human pace up the driveway to the quiet house.

I took a shaky breath as I watched him disappear through the door after a quick knock to announce his presence. As much as I knew we needed to deal with the threat of Bright before having *The Talk,* I found it very hard to suppress the warmth bubbling up from deep within every time I looked into either supe's eyes.

"So," The Shade said once Lightning was no longer in view, his voice unusually quiet. "You know who I am."

It took me a few seconds to realize what he meant, but when I did, the warmth in my body turned to icy fear. The phone call.

Being tortured had erased all my previous concern of what The Shade might do to me if my desperate plan to contact him worked. It obviously had, since they knew where to come looking for me, but I hadn't thought to tell Lightning so he could keep me safe. In fact, I'd let him walk away and leave me alone with The Shade, like an idiot.

I did my best to calm my suddenly racing heart and hoped that, if it turned out to be necessary, I would be able to shout loud enough to get Lightning's attention. Without looking away from the house, I said, "Yes."

The Shade was silent so long that the pounding of my heart seemed to be the only sound between us for five solid minutes.

Finally, I couldn't stand it anymore. I turned around slowly, as one would when in the company of a dangerous animal, and looked up into his eyes.

They were dark with some sort of emotion, but I couldn't make out what it was.

"Will you hurt me?" My voice was higher pitched than usual, and broke at the end.

Slowly, as if to not startle me, The Shade lifted a hand and let his thumb brush over my lower lip. The touch was gentle, but sent a shock of sensation through my entire body. "Never."

I probably shouldn't have pushed my luck, but the flood of relief—and, frankly, surprise—made me blurt out, "Why not?" Then, when I realized what I'd said, I continued, "I know your secret. I know I must be a liability now and—"

The Shade's thumb stopped my somewhat frantic stream of words.

"I *cannot* hurt you. You don't seem to understand that part. Even if I wanted to, harming you would be like hurting myself."

"Oh." I stared up at him, feeling oddly empty as I drank in the depths of his gaze. "Is that... is that part of the whole soulmate-thing Mirome spoke about?"

A small smile pulled his mouth up at the corners. "It would seem so."

"Oh," I repeated dumbly.

"Out of curiosity—what gave it away? When did you know?"

I lifted a finger to his mouth, gently touching the faint scar on his bottom lip. "Your scar. I saw it after you danced with me at the Autumn Ball, and recognized it from... from when you saved me."

"Hmm. I suppose you are the only one to ever see me that close in both disguises," he said.

We stood in silence for a bit, and The Shade's eyes drifted back to the house. Just when I thought he'd deemed the subject closed, he asked, "Have you told anyone?"

I frowned, a little taken aback that he would even think to ask, but then realized that he had to. In their world, betrayal was seemingly everywhere.

"No."

Another pause.

"Are you going to tell anyone?"

"No, Elias. Your secret is safe with me." Saying his name felt weird, but also oddly liberating. Up until now, my lovers had been masked, even while in bed with me, and when I'd cried out their names, it had been the alias they used to hide from the world. Calling The Shade by the name he used when he didn't don the mask was as intimate as feeling him press inside of me.

A ghost of a smile touched his scarred lip. "Eliath. My birth name is Eliath."

I would have said something more, asked him about his life as Elias, or Eliath, but before I could open my mouth, the front door we were booth looking at opened and Lightning stepped out. Alone.

By my side, the Shade tensed and muttered a foul curse, but it wasn't until Lightning got closer that I realized why.

Lightning's lips were pinched in a deep frown, and when he stopped in front of us, I realized that his suit had smears of blood covering his hands and arms.

"They're all dead," he said without preamble. "Bright killed the other Council members."

FOUR

KATHRYN

"Fuck!" The Shade flexed his massive hands and lifted his arms up behind his head, seemingly to avoid grabbing onto the nearest object and smashing it with frustration. "Crap!"

His outburst surprised me a little. "I'm sorry. Were you close?"

The Shade made a rude sound, but it was Lightning who explained.

"Hardly. But their death at Bright's hands means that what he's planning... it's bigger than we thought. He killed our leaders, Kat. This is not just war on the humans—it's a coup, a complete change in our society too. We've been governed by small councils in independent enclaves for centuries upon centuries. Bright killing St. Anthony's council... it will have worldwide consequences."

"And *we* have to stop him," The Shade spat. "Alone."

Oh. "Can't you contact some of the other supes? In other cities? If this will affect everyone, they might want to help."

"We can't," Lightning said. "We have no direct line of contact, so we would need to spend a few days finding out who was in charge there and how to contact them. Then spend however many days it would take to convince them that we were telling the truth. If Bright's killed our leaders, he's at the final stage of his plan. We have maybe a day or two to act before he plays his final move. If we want any chance at stopping him, we have to get to him before then."

"Okay," I said, reaching a hand out for each supe. "Let's go visit Mayor Wilkins."

THE MAYOR'S mansion was eerily quiet. Lightning and The Shade teleported us to a balcony opposite the side facing the street to avoid alerting guards or random passersby, but the silence from the big building seemed to be complete.

"Is it always so quiet?" I asked. My only real experience with the mansion came from when I'd attended the Autumn Ball, where there had been hundreds of people milling around both inside and out. Perhaps it was normally this abandoned, outside of major parties.

"No," Lightning mumbled, effectively killing off my hopeful theory in its infancy. "Something's definitely up. Stay alert."

The last bit was undoubtedly directed at The Shade, but I took it in nonetheless as we snuck in through the French doors and through the darkened room.

Lightning took the lead, I assumed because he had plenty of experience making his way through the mayor's mansion from previous visits. Even though we walked quietly and carefully along the many hallways, we never heard a single person, and the eerie feeling of wrongness increased for every minute.

Finally, Lightning stopped in front of the double doors I vaguely recognized from my visit to Wilkins' office.

Lightning looked over his shoulder at The Shade, nodding at some sort of signal from the other man, before he reached out and grabbed the handle, yanking open one of the doors.

It swung open, revealing the mayor behind his desk.

I blinked in surprise, even as The Shade shoved me inside and closed the door behind us. Somehow, the quietude of the mansion made me expect to find the office as empty as the rest of the house.

Mayor Wilkins looked up from the documents he was signing, a small smile gracing his lips at the sight of us. "Shade, Lightning. I see the rumors *are* true, then. You are working together these days. How... peculiar." He put the pen down and opened a drawer in his desk.

I don't know if it was the cool calculation in his voice, or the way he seemed so completely calm at our unexpected entrance, but finally, all the pieces clicked together in my brain. The threads that all led back to the mayor, without ever leaving a clear trail to exactly *how* he was connected to Bright. It was because we had never even thought to look at the only explanation that made sense.

"He is Bright." My startled whisper broke through the tension in the room as clearly as if I'd shouted it. "It's him."

Both Lightning and The Shade cast me a sharp glance, and I could see the realization breaking on their faces in the same split-second. They snapped their attention back on the mayor, The Shade sliding his twin swords out of the scabbards mounted on his back as they both moved into a defensive position in front of me.

Wilkins' smile broadened. "Oh, so *that's* what you see in the little cunt! She's the brain in your weird little triad. I mean, I'm sure Mirome's right about all his mate-babbling, too, the way you both act like she's Vasharyn incarnate, but I was so hoping it was more than just the magic. I'd just like to think that two of our greatest were brought to their knees by more than their cocks, you know?"

"I think you're mistaken, Bright," The Shade growled. "It seems you're the one who's about to be brought to his knees."

"We're going to end you, here and now," Lightning said, the lethal threat as chill-inducing as The Shade's roughened voice. "Whatever sick plan you have for overthrowing everything our race has fought for since our fall, it ends tonight."

Bright's laughter rang through the office, piercing and cold. "Oh, you pitiful fools. That's exactly what I'm going to correct. We will rise again!"

Faster than my human eyes could follow, he reached into the drawer under his desk and pulled out a big and unnervingly familiar gun. The one he'd used to commit a robbery with last year—the one Shaw Industries had unwittingly funded.

"Get down!" Lightning roared, and suddenly he flattened me against the floor with his body. A blue plasma burst exploded behind us, ripping the door to shreds with a boom that made my ears ring and my vision blur. The stench of burnt wood and varnish permeated the air.

"Stay down," Lightning hissed above me. Then he jumped up and launched himself at Bright. A dark shadow rushed toward them as The Shade joined the fight.

My heart pounded in my throat as the battle raged

around me, but at least Wilkins didn't fire the gun again. I dared to roll over from my prone position against the expensive rug to search for an escape route now that the door was no longer blocking the exit—and froze cold.

Behind the wreckage of the door stood row after row of masked people. From my low vantage point I couldn't make out how far back they went, but they were many. Far too many.

I croaked in an attempt at warning Lightning and The Shade, but I only got a hoarse gulp out before strong fingers closed around my throat, ending my outburst with a strangled wheeze.

Someone picked me up by my neck, cutting off my oxygen supply completely. My eyes bulged and my head pounded as I scratched and kicked and clawed at whoever had a hold of me, but I never so much as dented the suit they were wearing.

Just as I thought I was going to black out, they let go. I fell to the floor with a thud, but I was too busy sucking in air through my bruised throat to mind the pain when my knees impacted with the rug. Then someone grabbed my hair and pulled my head back, pressing a cold blade against my throat.

It was as if someone had hit the "pause" button on the scene in front of me. Both The Shade and Lightning stopped mid-fight, freezing in place as they took in the supe army behind me. I could practically see the frantic calculations behind their blue eyes as they tried to work out if they could somehow beat the odds.

"Oops! I forgot to mention we'd get company, didn't I?" Bright casually strolled around my two lovers so he could stand next to me and whoever had a knife to my throat. "Well, boys... I suppose this is checkmate, huh? Now, what was it we talked about before...? Oh yes, that's right—*kneel!* Kneel for me, or your human dies."

Both men dropped to their knees as if an invisible blade had cut the strings holding them up. Where I'd expected rage to flame from their eyes, I only saw desperation and mind numbing fear when our gazes met.

"Don't hurt her. Please—don't hurt her," The Shade rasped. All his normal power and grit seemed to have drained from his voice.

"I'll do anything," Lightning whispered next to him. "You win."

The sight of the powerful men throwing away their pride without another thought made the moisture in my eyes from the painful pull on my hair overflow and roll down my cheeks. It finally clicked that, however confusing and scary I found my feelings for both men, it was nothing compared to what they had gone through since marking me. If two of the most powerful superhumans in the city would kneel for their shared enemy and beg for him to spare me in front of so many others of their kind, whatever magic was in our bond had altered them both on a deep and fundamental level.

I didn't know much about their kind, but I'd learned that their pride was not something they took lightly. And yet here they were, on their knees begging for my life.

"Well, whether or not she gets hurt is entirely dependent on you. Let's play a little game, shall we?" Bright took a few steps forward and pointed his gun at them.

"Which one of you will give your life for hers? I will release the girl to the other and let them leave the city."

Before I'd fully grasped the significance of his words, both men had gotten to their feet, but Lightning placed a hand on

The Shade's chest and shook his head. "No." Without another look at his old enemy, he stepped forward and stared Bright straight in the eyes. "I will give my life for hers, if I have your word—with all our Brothers and Sisters as witnesses—that you will let her leave with The Shade, unharmed."

Bright moved the gun to aim at Lightning. "You have my word, *hero.*"

"No, Lightning!" It finally, fully set in what he was doing. Everything in my body screamed in protest at the thought of losing him, and I knew without a doubt that I wouldn't live through seeing him killed. "No, no! Don't do this!" I fought against the supe who held me with all my strength, but all it earned me was more pain from my scalp and throat, until I was completely and efficiently immobilized by someone else grabbing my arm and twisting it up high on my back.

"It's okay, Kittykat," Lightning said, his voice much calmer now than when he had pleaded for my life. "It's for the best."

"How can you dying be for the best? No, I won't let you!" I cried as the panic raged in my body and made it hard to breathe. I couldn't lose him, I couldn't lose any of them. I'd rather die myself. "I won't!"

"You don't have a choice," Bright sneered. "The mighty hero has finally achieved his life goal and gotten the chance to give up his very existence for the humans he loves so dearly. We can't take that from him. Seize him!"

A few supes broke out from the cluster behind me and grabbed Lightning by the arms, pulling him the final few steps in front of Bright and forcing him to his knees again. But he didn't look at the villain with the gun aimed at his chest—he looked at me, and the love in his eyes took my breath away.

"I love you, Kathryn, with everything that I am. I am so sorry I let the fear of our bond come between getting to know you for who you truly are—my soulmate. That's why it has to be me. The Shade never had any reservations, and as much as I hate him, I know he will do everything in his power to keep you happy and safe. That's all that matters."

"No," I sobbed again, trying to blink away the tears that were now coming hard and fast. "I love you too. I can't live without you."

"Yes, you can," Lightning said. "And you will. I know you love him, too. You will get through this together and live a long and happy life."

"Yes, well, this is all very touching and stuff," Bright interrupted "but I have a city to conquer, and a superhero to defame in front of millions of anxious citizens. To be quite honest, the thought of seeing the hope of salvation from their beloved Lightning crushed in all their little faces when I dangle you from the rooftop makes me kinda giddy. But first, how about we all see who hides behind the mask, shall we?"

Lightning held my gaze as Bright reached down and grasped at his mask. The villain pulled, ripping the fabric as he removed the cover that hid Lightning's true identity from the world.

Blond hair spilled out, framing high cheekbones and a very familiar square jaw.

My quiet gasp was echoed from behind me, because even though his eyes were still glowing blue with the mark of a superhuman, there was no mistaking the man kneeling in front of the corrupt mayor. Nick Coleman, the city's most famous reporter—the man who spent his professional life fighting for the weakest members of society.

It wasn't just when he was wearing the mask he worked for justice and protection of humans—it wasn't just about some secret agenda to gain favor with the city. Lightning—Nick—was good, to his very core, despite his cocksure attitude.

And now, he had finally sacrificed everything he could. For me.

"Ha! Oh, this is too good!" Bright's triumphant laugh cut through my shock, rang through the office, and drowned out the surprised mumbles from the superhumans behind me. "Of course you're Nick-freaking-Coleman. Saving pitiful humans by night wasn't enough, was it? Ha! If there ever was more of a poster boy for foolhardiness, I haven't met him! This is going to be so good. You know what, I think we'll make a slight change in tonight's plans. We'll have Nick Coleman explain to the good people of St. Anthony how they are now slaves for their new masters. That should go down a little easier, shouldn't it, *Nick?*"

Lightning finally looked away from me to level a glare at Bright. "I have no idea how you think your sick plan will ever work. There's a reason no one's tried this since we lost our original form, *Wilkins*. The humans far outnumber us. You know this. You are leading our Brothers and Sisters to their deaths. You may slaughter thousands of humans, but ultimately, they will win."

This time, Bright's laugh was so cold, so dark, it raised goosebumps all along my arms and back. "But that's the beautiful part. That's what makes my plan so *brilliant*, if I do say so myself. I have found a way for us to ascend, as the true

Masters of the World we were meant to be. By daybreak tomorrow, we will rise as dragons again!"

Whoa. *Dragons?* They were *dragons?* Dragons were a thing? Despite the horrific situation we were in, some part of my brain had enough energy left to be surprised.

Cheering erupted from the group behind me, victorious whoops mixing with the chorus, making it clear that every last one of them were here for the promise of gaining their dragon form, however that was possible.

"Speaking of daybreak," Bright shouted above the cheering. "Brothers, Sisters—it is time! Grab the traitor and let's get moving! And you—" The last part was aimed at The Shade, who had kept quiet during the full exchange. "If you want to live happily ever after with the human, you best take her now and get out of the city. After tonight, it won't welcome anyone who ever opposed our true rule."

The supe who'd kept me immobilized up until that point shoved me forward and into The Shade's embrace. He closed his arms around me in a steel cage of protection and turned, letting me see Lightning one last time as the supes pulled him out of the ruined door to his doom.

Then I felt a pull behind my navel and the world vanished into swirling darkness.

FIVE

THE SHADE

Eliath watched in silence as Kathryn stumbled the few feet from his embrace to his bed after the teleport. She sat down as abruptly as if her legs gave in.

He had taken her to his penthouse—the one no one ever came to, because it was the one place in the world he knew was safe. No supe knew this place belonged to him. Now that Lightning was gone, there was no longer a need to stay on the neutral grounds of her apartment.

Dammit! The knowledge that he could now keep her in his own domain should have brought nothing but pleasure, as should the fact that he no longer had any competition for her. How fucking typical of Lightning to ruin what should have been a perfectly good triumph with his *noble heroics*.

His archenemy had sacrificed himself so that she could have a future with Eliath—even though Eliath had stepped forward, too.

The place behind his ribs, where he felt the connection from the mark he'd put on Kathryn keenly, ached at the realization that Lightning had as much as given him his damn

41

blessing to ride off into the sunset with the woman they both wanted as their own. They had been bitter enemies for so many years now, the idea that Lightning's last free act had been to give Eliath the one thing he wanted more than he had ever wanted anything else in his life was unfathomable. Even if the sacrifice had been for Kathryn, more than it had been for him.

A soft sniffle from the bed brought him out of his musings, and his heart spasmed unpleasantly when he realized Kathryn was crying.

Damn Lightning and his ability to make what *should* have been the best fucking day of his life utterly miserable.

She loved Lightning—there was no doubt in his heart, not after seeing them in bed together and hearing her sobbed confession today. And as for Lightning, he had clearly also given in to the idea of them being soulmates, rather than it being the instinctive urge to breed messing with their magic core.

Eliath scrubbed his hands over his face, and then pulled the mask off. There was no need anymore. Kathryn knew his true face, and there was no need to hide who he was from her.

His old enemy had been right about one thing, at least. There was nothing he wouldn't do for the woman quietly crying on his bed, even fleeing his city and his position here.

Eliath sank down on the bed next to Kathryn and wrapped his arms around her so he could pull her in close. He didn't have much experience with comforting weeping women, but it felt instinctive to hold her and offer his strength to her.

She pressed against him, clutching tightly to his chest, which seemed to confirm his reaction as the right move. It also made his cock rise, as if awakened by the sheer proximity of her.

Eliath suppressed a groan and shifted his hips as to not prod her with his erection. As much as he enjoyed being buried inside of her, he didn't think she'd take too kindly to his shifting focus in the middle of her tears.

Kathryn looked up then, and he prepared himself for her outrage. But she just reached up a hand and stroked the side of his face, letting her fingertips trail up over his shaved scalp, exploring his face as if she was seeing it for the first time. Which, in a way, she was. He hadn't bothered suppressing his naturally glowing eye color as he normally did when in his human disguise. No one had seen him like this since his parents died.

"He's gone," she said, her voice wavering a little. "Lightning's gone."

Eliath didn't reply, didn't know what to say to ease her grief. His own tumultuous feelings on the subject were much too confusing—and surprising—to work out, so he wasn't exactly qualified to help her with hers. Instead, he cupped the back of her head in one hand and stroked her tangled hair gently, hoping his physical presence would be enough for her to find some comfort.

Much to his surprise, it seemed to be. Without warning, Kathryn reached up and pulled his head down with both hands before pressing her mouth to his in a desperate kiss. Her lips separated as she gasped for breath against him and her fingers dug into his skull until he let his mouth mirror hers. She tasted salty from her tears, but he didn't mind. Kissing Kathryn was only second to fucking her, and he relished the rush of ecstasy brought on by losing himself in her kiss.

It was impossible for him to not feel her desperation to forget the pain from losing Lightning, even if it was just for a little while, but he invited the oblivion with open arms. When he was with her like this, nothing else mattered, and she wasn't the only one who craved a few moments relief from any and all thoughts.

"I need you," she gasped against his lips when he pulled back to let her suck in a few breaths of air. "Please, I need you."

He had heard her say those words before, but this time, it was different. It wasn't as much the sex she needed as the assurance of their connection. He knew, because her plea resonated with the inexplicable void in his own chest left behind by Lightning's sacrifice.

Eliath growled low in his throat, only too keen to escape the complicated emotions by burying himself inside of his woman. His cock throbbed painfully, as if her plea had gone directly to his crotch—which, judging by what little experience he had with her, it might well have. His suit suddenly felt unbearably restrictive. With another growl he ripped it off, not caring if he burst a few seams, and then descended on her already shredded clothes.

Kathryn squirmed against him as he tore at her shirt, easing his quest to get her naked as best she could. When she was completely bared to him she wrapped her arms around his body again.

Eliath caught a groan in his throat when he felt her tightened nipples press into his chest, followed by the soft press of her full breasts. He slid his hands down over the generous swell of her hips and pressed her closer still, losing himself in softness of her curves. Her naked flesh against his was the sweetest sensation he'd ever known, equally arousing and comforting.

"Eliath," she murmured before stretching to nibble his earlobe. An electric jolt shot through his nervous system in response, ramping up his urges. This time, he didn't manage to keep the groan in. She made that soft noise that always drove him wild when he caught her lips in a scorching kiss. His hands were pressing her down on her back before he'd made the conscious decision to move things to the next stage. It was always like that with his Kitten—his animal instincts were in the driver's seat from the moment her intoxicating presence overpowered him, until he spilled himself deep in her womb.

Eliath crawled in over her, capturing her lips again, but she soon pulled back from his kiss and pressed his head further down. He smirked and let her, only too happy to obey. When he closed his lips around a pert nipple Kathryn moaned and spread her legs in invitation. He let his fingers trail down to the thatch of hair and split her lower lips with a couple of fingers, testing how close she was.

As always, she was soaking for him even before he'd gotten to tease her. His cock pulsed with need, urging him to ignore further preparations. She would be able to take him now, even if her pussy would protest his size for the first few thrusts. He knew from their previous couplings that she liked when he was forceful, preferred it even, but this time they both needed more than hard and rough.

With a gentle stroke Eliath slid his fingers up to her clit as he sucked harder on her breast. Kathryn's breath exploded out of her lungs and her back arched. He loved how responsive she was, though it made it even harder for him to control of his urge to flip her over and rut her like a beast.

Teasingly, he swept his tongue around her nipple, flicking it a few times while he gently rubbed her clit until he could feel her muscles tense and relax in rhythm with her hard gasps. Then he switched to her other breast at the same time as he let a couple of fingers slip inside her tight sheath, rotating his hand so he could continue rubbing circles against her clit with his thumb.

"*Ohh!*" Her moan went straight to his cock. *Fuck,* he wanted to be inside of her more than anything else. His fingers were covered in her slickness and clutched tightly by her internal muscles, reminding him all too well of what it felt like when it was his cock forcing her wide.

Eliath lifted up off Kathryn, ignoring her protests as his hand came away from her entrance. Gone were any thoughts of this being more than primitive needs needing to be quenched—whatever it was they were both yearning for, they would have to find it while he drove into her as deep as she would take him.

But when he knelt between her thighs, the intoxicating scent of her pussy washed over his face. Eliath groaned with want and, before he knew it, he was flat on his stomach between her thighs with his face pressed to the source of her very being.

Superhuman pheromones were said to affect humans quite strongly, but he doubted anyone had ever been as addicted as he was to this little human's scent.

Kathryn moaned and squirmed as he lapped at her soaking slit. When he found her clit and flicked it teasingly, her nails found his scalp and dug in. It might have hurt, had he not been so high on lust, but now, it only made him all the more determined. He captured the stiff little bud between his teeth and bit down ever so gently.

The effect was immediate. Kathryn screamed and tried to clamp her thighs together at the intense burst of sensation, but he forced them open wide again with both hands and wrapped his lips around her clit, sucking deeply.

It worked as intended.

Kathryn's scream broke off into a high-pitched whimper. Her entire body convulsed once, twice, three times until he relented, licking her with broad, full strokes as she rocked against him, moaning incoherently. The tang of her climax bathed his tongue and made his vision blacken with the intensity of his own need. But he wasn't stopping his worship of her, not until—

"Enough. Please, stop!" Where she had clutched him to her before, she now frantically tried to shove his head away from her oversensitive flesh.

Eliath complied and pulled back. Her sex glistened with her fluids and his saliva, and the petals leading the way to her innermost sanctuary were open in invitation. He breathed in deeply in an attempt to let her rest before demanding his own pleasure, but that only gave him a face-full of her delicious pheromones.

He moved without conscious thought, climbed on top of her and spread her thighs wide with his own so he could nestle his hips in between them. His cockhead parted her lower lips without effort, and then he was met with her tight, incredible heat.

"Fuck!" he snarled as the connection with her snapped into place the second her tight pussy wrapped around his flared tip. An electric current traveled all the way up his spine. *More;* he needed more.

"Oh, God! Fuck!" Kathryn braced her hands against his shoulders, slowing his penetration. It took all he had not to just slam in to the hilt, but for once, he obeyed her attempt at setting the pace.

The result was exquisite. As much as he loved ravaging her soft, little body until his nearly unquenchable thirst for her was sated, there was something utterly perfect about the slow slide into the depths of her very core. He felt every ripple in her channel, every twitching muscle as he drove in. Her face alone was a study in tense pleasure. Looking into her eyes as he filled her made something from the place he was connected to her by the mark reach out, as if to penetrate her very soul like he did her body.

When he was finally fully seated inside of her, the world held still for three long seconds—until she raised her hips to urge him on and shredded his self-restraint.

"Yes!" She gasped her approval out as he moved, slid her arms around him, and held on as if he was the most important person in the whole world. He was vaguely aware of his own grunts and moans for every time he bottomed out in her, but mostly, he was lost in her eyes and the eternal clenching of her pussy around his thick cock.

Eliath was so consumed, he didn't think to protest when she nudged his shoulder and rolled him over, slipping off his hard length as she moved. He just allowed her to push him, until suddenly he found himself on his back with her straddling his hips, the length of his cock pressing hard against her stomach.

Her mouth split in a teasing smile, and he realized his facial expression must have shown some measure of shock. He *was* pretty shocked—as far back as he could recall, he had never let another put him in a submissive position before, not inside nor outside of the bedroom. He was always in control, always the dominant party in any situation—*always*. Every instinct in his preternatural body should have been roaring to roll her back over and punish her long and hard for her nerve, but all he could think about was how much he needed to be back inside of her, position be damned.

"You look like I just pulled out a strap-on," Kathryn said, sliding her hands up his tense muscles in a half-soothing, half-inciting caress. She rocked her hips, rubbing her clit against his cock, and moaned at the contact. "Don't tell me this is your first time getting ridden."

"Get on it, woman, or you're getting flipped over," he growled, his patience rapidly declining for every second he was left without her wet embrace.

Kathryn smiled and raised up higher on her knees, nestling Eliath's pulsing cockhead against her slick entrance. Slowly, so slowly—he had to bury his hands in the sheets to stop himself from grabbing onto her hips and forcing her down—she took him in. Her tight heat never stopped sinking, until finally, he was all the way in and she was resting against his groin, breathing deeply from the pressure.

When she began moving, he tore the sheets to shreds.

It was so different than what he had known up until now, the way her muscles moved around his cock as she rose and fell on him, pulling him closer to his release rather than allowing him to chase it. Eliath groaned and panted, caught between his desire to let her ride him so he could enjoy the agonizingly slow climb, and the primal urge to reach the blissful end.

The sight of her full tits bouncing for each downward slope made him decide on some sort of a compromise.

Eliath pushed himself up into a seated position, leaning on one arm so he could wrap the other around her back and pull her close. He bent his head and caught a nipple between his lips, and then started moving his pelvis in rhythm with hers, meeting her every downward movement with an upward thrust of his own.

Kathryn gasped at the added friction, which only encouraged him to pound into her harder. Her gasps quickly turned to cries, and when her fingernails dug into his shoulders, drawing blood, he lost the final vestiges of his self-control. Eliath rolled her over onto her back and raised up over her writhing body on his hands so he could finally fuck her as hard as his instincts demanded. From the way her tight sheath spasmed for every thrust, he knew she would soon reach her climax even without having her clit stimulated, but he shifted his weight onto one hand and moved the other down to her small pearl, nonetheless. Nothing felt better on his cock than when his Kitten came from his dual assault on her frantic little pussy.

"Fuck! Eliath!" Kathryn's entire body seized in a tight arch underneath him.

Eliath growled in response. Her pussy milked him hard and relentlessly, bringing his own climax on in a torrent of unbearable ecstasy. He slammed in one more time, pressing his flared cockhead so deep his cock found heaven as the first spurt of his release flooded into her.

There was nothing but her, nothing but the pleasure wracking through his very being from where they were connected. Mindlessly, he moved in her a few more times until all he had and all he was was spent inside of her.

Eliath collapsed on top of Kathryn, only barely remembering to catch himself so he didn't flatten her with his much greater body mass. Little bursts of electricity crawled along his skin, rendering him as vulnerable as a newborn lamb. How did she *do* that? Sex was not meant to be such a near-fucking-*spiritual* experience, he was sure of it. That, or he had been doing it wrong for most of his life.

"I love you."

The quiet whisper from underneath him made his orgasm-blissed brain snap back into focus so instantly it almost hurt. Surprised, he turned his head to look at Kathryn's pretty face. It was flushed and sweaty with exertion as expected, but she was also staring at him with an odd mix of exhilaration and fear, where normally, she'd be too high on her orgasm to look anything but content. Yup, he'd heard right.

"I love you, too."

Perhaps he should have spent some time angsting over whether or not what he felt for her was anything more than primal magic forcing them together, as Mirome claimed, but as he looked into her eyes, the words came of their own accord. And he knew them to be true—as true as anything in his life had ever been. He loved her, with all that he was, because she was his soulmate. Simple as that.

That's why, when her face contorted in pain and she began crying against his shoulder, he knew that their love would never be whole again without the other third of their unity.

Yes, he loved her with every fiber of his being, because as he held her close to soothe her heartache, he knew without a doubt he would do anything in his power to return Lightning to them. Even betray everything his race had held sacred for millennia.

SIX

KATHRYN

I was thankful that Eliath didn't just get up the second I started bawling like a baby.

What a way to react to hearing what I'd been so desperate to hear, even if I'd spent a good amount of time in complete denial. He loved me too. Eliath loved me, like I loved him. It was time to put on my big-girl panties and honor Lightning's sacrifice.

I did my best to wipe away my tears and swallow down the sobs that kept pressing against the inside of my chest like hot, aching bubbles of despair. "We should really get going, Eliath. If Bright's plan is unfolding at dawn, we need to get out now, get as far away as possible before it happens."

He looked down at me for a moment, and I could practically see the calculations behind his glowing, blue eyes. He was up to something.

I raised an eyebrow at him. "What?"

Carefully, so my body had time to adjust, Eliath raised up off me and pulled out, grunting when his softened cock slipped from my swollen pussy. I cringed at the sensation of his semen rushing out from the deepest part of my channel and silently thanked the Lord that I'd been smart enough to get on birth control early on. Somehow, I had an idea that superhumans also had super-strong sperm, if my reaction to a mouthful of Lightning's was anything to go by.

"You don't know what will happen if Wilkins truly succeeds in giving back his followers their dragon form, Kitten," he said as he slumped down on the bed and rolled over so he could look at me, one hand propping up his head. "In ancient times, we ruled the human territories we conquered without mercy. No weaponry could stand against our power, and we were ... less human than we are today. Less compassionate. If Wilkins succeeds, not only will the entire population of St. Anthony be slaves—he and his followers will be merciless. They will kill, torture, and rape for sport, and no one will be able to stop them."

Guilt swept over me at the thought of what would happen to all the people in the city—*my* city—if no one stopped Bright. But what could we do? We had tried to stop him, and we had lost.

"Why did your ancestors ever give up your dragon forms in the first place?" I asked. "If you were so much more powerful as dragons?"

"We were very few, back then. Maybe a dozen, and very territorial. They got bored of their self-imposed solitude and started to take on the guise of human flesh to be able to walk among them. Some started to get involved in human politics, pulling on strings behind the curtain and playing with mighty rulers as if they were puppets," Eliath said, distractedly drawing circles with a finger on my naked hip as he explained.

"I see that's nothing new, then," I muttered. "How did you end up stuck in human form, then?"

Eliath sighed. "Hubris, of course. They got too careless, believing themselves all-powerful, taking risks where they shouldn't have. And then, one day, the humans realized that their highest posts had been infiltrated, and killed one of our oldest ancestors in his human form. Up until then, no one knew how vulnerable the human disguise was. The humans captured the Queen of Dragons before she could shift and forced her to perform a spell that ensured no dragon could ever return to their natural form.

"It's one of the stories we all learn at our mother's teat—where we come from and how we lost it. And I believe that's why Bright has been able to overthrow all our customs and laws—most of us yearn for our ancestral power, as we were taught to do, not realizing that the world has changed so much since then. We are far too many to share the world like our ancestors did, and the humans have had millennia to forget that they have not always been the master race. It will turn into war and destruction, and more than likely, the whole planet will burn."

"Well, look at The Big, Bad Shade being Mr. Rational," I said. "There was a time I would have thought you'd be in front of the line to gain that sort of power."

Eliath gave me a ghost of a smile. "Perhaps. I was quite content ruling the business world by day, and the banks by night, though. And now... now, there's you. It's one of the tales that seems to have been kept hidden—how our ancestors intermingled with humans and spread their genes. Only the Secret Keeper knows that every once in a while, a human and a dragonborn are connected by their very souls, allowing for a union." He lifted his hand from my hip and touched my face gently. The smolder in his eyes made my heart flutter and my abdomen clench wantonly, despite still being a bit sore from our recent activities.

"What, exactly, is a Secret Keeper?" I asked in an attempt at distracting my lower region. Now was not the time for an encore.

"There is only one at any time. It is the one who carries all our secrets, all our old tales and history, in their mind. Once they are killed, he or she who kills the old Secret Keeper will take over the mantle. As I understand it, the old Keeper's knowledge will transfer at the moment of death, bestowing it onto the new host. What they then choose to do with it is up to them. Some have kept their status hidden, some have come forward to help govern our path and shape our society. Mirome is the current Secret Keeper—my best guess, he's the one who has convinced Bright that there is a way to regain our dragon form. But at least he also did something good. He's the one who told us about human mates... though he failed to understand the true meaning of what's between you and I, and Lightning. He called it breeding instincts, purely based on the need for our magic to spread, but that's because he didn't understand—*couldn't* understand—what meeting your true mate is like.

"Kathryn... you are my soul. And you are Lightning's soul. It is that simple. Which means that, without him, *we* won't be complete. Ever."

My lower lip trembled at his words, and I had to bite it not to start crying again—because, in the deepest part of my being, I knew he was right. I didn't understand dragon magic, or what made people soulmates, but I knew that Lightning and The Shade—Nick and Eliath—were two of the three parts my very foundation was made up of.

Not that it changed the cold, hard facts.

I set my jaw and blinked the moisture out of my eyes.

"Lightning gave his life for us, Eliath. His *life*. The only thing worse than losing him would be if we didn't honor his sacrifice. We have to try to make a life for ourselves, and to do that, we need to leave St. Anthony—right now."

Eliath leaned over and placed a kiss on my lips. It was warm and comforting, but chaste. Without moving his head back more than a millimeter so he could lock his eyes in mine, he asked, "Do you really think I would accept that my soulmate will never be truly happy? You need Lightning. And, though I don't share your sentimental attachment to the wretched people in this city, I know the slaughter of them would haunt you for an eternity, what with that annoying 'good soul' flaw you seem to have been burdened with. I'm not going to allow you a lifetime of sorrow, Kathryn. I can't. Which means I'll stay. And fight."

As much as his love shone through every word, and everything in me desperately wanted to cling to the promise and conviction in his voice, I shook my head. "You can't. I can't lose you too. I won't."

"Kathryn." Eliath stroked my cheek and tipped my chin up when I tried to look away. "I am not what you'd call a 'noble soul'. I'm not saying this to go and martyr myself in some battle for the greater good of humankind. And, frankly, I don't much care for Lightning. I'd be perfectly happy with leaving this rotten city behind, take you somewhere far, far away where Bright and his followers will never come, and stay there and make lots of babies with you until the end of our days. And, if you tell me you believe you can ever be truly happy knowing that the city went up in smoke and your other soulmate is dead, then that's exactly what I'll do.

"So tell me, my Kitten... can you?"

Perhaps in another state of mind, the "lots of babies" part would have warranted a comment or two, but at that point, all I could do was shake my head as my tears finally won the battle over my willpower.

"Then that's settled," Eliath said. He kissed my forehead and then rolled over and climbed out of bed.

I watched him pull on his clothes, for once not hypnotized by the flexing of his hard stacks of muscles. "But how? There are no superhumans left in the city who will stand against Bright, and you said yourself that getting help from other enclaves in time was impossible."

Eliath's mouth set in a grim line as he pulled on his mask, once again looking like the villain who had first claimed me. "No. There are no supes left. But there are others in this city who would fight against Bright, if they knew what he's got planned."

SEVEN

KATHRYN

"Are you sure about this?" I asked. "Maybe I should go in alone."

Eliath rolled his eyes. "Yes, I'm sure, Kitten. You think the Chief of Police would believe some random girl walking in off the street? It has to be me."

"It's not like you got the most trustworthy of reputations," I muttered as he grabbed me around the waist.

Eliath ignored me. The now familiar sensation of a pull by my navel made me clench my teeth, and then the world fell in on itself.

We appeared with a *crack* in the middle of an office. I bent double to dry-heave until the bout of nausea eased, so I missed the Chief of Police's initial reaction to our unexpected arrival.

I didn't miss the metallic click of a gun being cocked.

Slowly, I straightened up with both hands in the air, but the man on the other side of the worn desk didn't even look at me. His eyes were glued to my large companion, lips pulled back from his teeth in what could have been anger, but the trembling of his hands as he clutched his weapon gave away his fear.

"I don't know what you want, Shade, but you just made a grave mistake."

Eliath sighed, deeply and rather provokingly, considering he had a loaded gun pointed straight at his chest. "You and I both know you can't fire that thing before I've snapped your wrist." His eyes narrowed a fraction as the chief's lips opened halfway. "Don't be stupid. If you call on anyone, I'm just going to have to bring you somewhere more private—perhaps the top of the City Bank? You and I do have a lot of history with that building, after all. Put down your weapon and sit down, Chief. I'm only here to talk."

The chief didn't look like he appreciated being told to sit down in his own office, but he obeyed nonetheless, after clearly weighing the truth of the villain's words. He sat down on his chair, his entire posture so rigid I imagined he'd need a serious massage after this visit. The glare he leveled at Eliath could have made lesser men wither on the spot.

"I'm here because the city is in danger," Eliath began, casually taking a seat in front of the chief's desk without having been invited. "And I realize you're now planning on spending a good half hour telling me why you have no reason to trust my word for anything, probably spiced up with a few choice profanities and insults. We don't have that kind of time, I'm afraid, so let's just fast-forward to where you tell me what will make you believe me, so we can save this wretched city from the biggest fucking catastrophe it will ever face, before time's up and everyone's either dead or enslaved."

The Chief opened and closed his mouth a few times, and

I silently cringed at Eliath's disrespect. He hadn't even bothered to tell the man what was happening.

"Sir, many of the superhumans have organized, with Bright leading them. They are planning on taking over the city and enslaving all of us." I stepped forward from my spot halfway behind Eliath to get the chief's attention, though I didn't have the gall to sit down in the last empty chair without an invitation. When his eyes flickered from Eliath's masked face to me, I continued. "It's not a joke, sir. It's happening tonight, and if we don't do something, the entire city will be lost."

The chief frowned at me. "And let's say for a moment that I believe you, and this 'thing' is actually happening. How did you two come about this information? And who, exactly, are you, miss?"

"My name is Kathryn Smith, and I'm a bl—a freelance journalist. I've been investigating corruption in the mayor's office for several weeks now, and that's how I came across this." I cleared my throat when the chief gave me a questioning look before glancing at the villain. "Yes, well... that's how I met The Shade, too. He was looking into Bright's operations and our trails crossed."

I realized that, to the rest of the world, the man who called himself my soulmate maintained a reputation as a ruthless killer, and knew I had to add a bit of drama to my explanation if I wanted any chance of the Chief to believe me.

"When he saw what I'd uncovered and that I could be useful, he decided I could be useful. So I've been working with... uh, *for* him since, in an effort to uncover what was happening. Sir, we found out that Bright and Mayor Wilkins are one and the same."

"And, as I said, he's planning on quite literally killing or enslaving every single human in this city within the next few hours, so could we please skip to the part where you tell me what will need to happen for you to round up your officers and help me stop him?" Eliath interrupted. "Because if we don't get moving soon, it'll be too late."

"How about proof?" The chief raised both eyebrows at the clearly agitated villain across his desk. "At this point, all I have is some unknown girl and the city's most wanted criminal making wild accusations. Forgive me if I'm not jumping at the chance to send my officers on a wild goose chase around town just on your word, Shade."

"Funny thing," Eliath growled. His agitation with not being immediately obeyed was clearly mounting. "When supervillains infiltrate your local government with plans to overthrow it, they rarely leave much proof behind until *after* it's done. But you want proof I'm not lying? Fine. Then let me give you the one thing I know you've been salivating for for the past decade, *Chief*."

Eliath's hands went to his face, but it wasn't until I saw him nimbly grasp his mask that I realized what he was doing.

He was ruining any chance of a life among humans—and probably throwing away his staggering fortune.

With a careless flick of his wrist, Eliath tossed his mask on the desk in front of him and looked at the stunned chief, eyebrows raised in challenge. "Ready to listen now?"

"I'll be damned." The Chief of Police stared at him, as if Eliath might vanish into thin air if he blinked. "Elias Shaw. Damn, that's..."

Eliath just stared back at him, waiting for him to process what I couldn't argue was quite a shock, having been on the receiving end of it myself.

To the chief's credit, it only took him a few moments. Then his gaze darkened as realization set in. "This is for real. Bright is really Mayor Wilkins, and he's planning on... on what, exactly? Tell me everything you've uncovered, to the smallest detail." He reached for his phone and leveled a hard stare at Eliath. "And then you will tell me everything there is to know about fighting superhumans. One wrong move on your part, and this time, I will know how to catch you."

"I NEVER KNEW how much of being a supe was about hanging out on random rooftops." I looked out across the city stretching out below us with. The multitude of lights looked almost pretty from up here, where the noise of the many people it shone for was only a faint buzz on the wind.

Eliath hugged me closer with a somewhat teasing grin, shielding me from the howling wind. "I know. Everyone expects glamour and champagne, but really, it's all about the stake-outs. At least it's not raining, eh?"

"Oh, yes, that would be what ruined this night. Rain." I squinted out into the dark. "Can you see anything noteworthy?"

"No." He rubbed a hand across his scalp and groaned with frustration. "We've been to every goddamn hot-spot for supes this town's got. Where the fuck are they hiding?"

"I dunno, where do crazy supes plotting to overthrow the human government tend to hang out? I'm guessing you have more experience with this sort of thing than—" I paused as Bright's gloating when he unmasked Lightning echoed for my inner ear. "He's at a news studio!"

Eliath frowned. "A news studio?"

"Yes! Remember how Bright said he'd use Lightning's—Nick's—face to tell the city about their new masters? Where else would he do that than from a news studio? Now we just have to figure out which one... how many are there in total in the city?" My excitement died somewhat. St. Anthony was a big city, with a very active media.

"Son of a *bitch!*" Eliath growled. "I know which one that little prick is at."

I raised my eyebrows at him, not quite following.

"He was banging your friend from the DNSA Network, and has infiltrated it deeply enough to cipher money from it too. The fucker is at *my* network."

"Of course!" I ignored the twinge at the mention of Trish. What I thought we'd had had been mostly a lie, at least for the past several years, and right now, I had to focus on the mission at hand.

Eliath tightened his grip around me, and once again I was pulled through what felt like a rip in the fabric of reality l. When the world re-focused, Eliath clamped a hand tightly over my mouth before I could even begin my usual dry-heaving. When it finally stopped, I realized we were standing on a narrow balcony on what looked to be sixth floor of one of the old and grand buildings at the town center.

When Eliath was sure I wouldn't retch, he removed his hand and pressed his lips to my ear. "They're down on third floor. I can hear Bright—and Lightning. I'm going to teleport us up to the roof so I can call the chief without anyone overhearing us. Hang tight."

This time, after we popped into view a few floors up, Eliath let me gag as he snatched his cell phone out of a hidden pocket and pressed a few buttons. Soon, he was speaking quickly and quietly into the device.

My stomach finished the most violent of its protests just as he wrapped up his conversation with the chief.

"They're on their way." Eliath crouched down next to where I was still standing, bent over, hands on my knees. My stomach was not happy with the amount of times I'd been teleported across town within the past twenty-four hours. "Kathryn... if this goes wrong..."

I shot him a dirty glare. "I'm not staying here while you go risk your life. We've talked about this."

"I know," he said, his unusually soft tone mirrored in his eyes. He reached out and stroked a hand through my tangled hair, wrapping his fingers around the back of my neck gently enough that it felt good. Safe. "And I remember the promise I made you about not sidelining you again. But, Kitten, if something happens to you down there... I wouldn't be able to survive it. Please, reconsider. For me."

It was hard to resist a plea like that from one of the two people I loved most in this world, but I knew I couldn't sit this one out. Even if every part of me dreaded what we were about to attempt.

"And you think *I* could survive if *you* died? You *and* Lightning? You say I'm your soulmate... does it not seem plausible that that's a two-way street? I—I don't know exactly how all this works and what it means, but I know that I love you... and that I wouldn't be able to make it without the both of you. *I* can't let *you* go down there on your own, don't you understand? They are so many, and they are so powerful... I may just be a human, but I am going to be there for you, Eliath. And for Lightning. They aren't expecting you to bring me there again. I'll sneak in without getting noticed. The only reason they got me before is because they ambushed us. Well, this time, it's the other way around."

Eliath held my gaze for a few seconds, as if it took him a little while to digest what I'd said. Then he pulled me closer by the back of my neck and pressed a kiss to my forehead. "Be safe. Always. Don't take any chances, no matter what, or who, is at stake. Do not feel pity, or remorse, or guilt—it will make you hesitate, and if you hesitate, you die. And if you die, so do I, and so does Lightning."

"No pressure," I muttered, trying to keep my voice from trembling.

Eliath reached behind his back and pulled a long, thin knife from one of the scabbards that holstered his swords. With a flick of his wrist he turned the handle toward me, holding it out in offering. "I wish we would have had time to teach you how to shoot, but since we haven't, this will be safer. Go for the eyes, throat, or up underneath the bottom rib. Don't go between—you risk the blade getting stuck on one. Strike to kill, not to wound. Remember, they are not human—an injury won't stop them, even if it looks severe. And Kathryn... your only advantage is to stay hidden until the very last second. If you get drawn out into the open, you don't stand a chance. *Stay hidden.* Got it?"

I nodded and took the blade. "I got it."

"I love you."

His grave tone sent chills up my spine, but I pushed all the horrible thoughts of what could go wrong away. It was too late for fear, and too late for regrets. "I love you too. So much."

Eliath nodded. "Okay. Let's do this." He turned his back to me and crouched down. "I'll climb down to make sure no one hears the teleport, so you'll have to get on my back. Hang on tight, and make sure you climb off without a sound when we reach the balcony on the third floor. We'll wait for the police to arrive and then I'm going in, hopefully taking them by surprise enough that I can get to Bright. You will *stay hidden* on the balcony until you are *absolutely sure* you can sneak in unnoticed. See if you can get to Lightning. He's undoubtedly restrained. Get him free as soon as possible. We'll need as much power as we can get. Ready?"

I swallowed thickly, secured the knife in my coat pocket, and climbed onto Eliath's broad back. The feel of his strong muscles flexing underneath my grip was oddly reassuring. We might be outnumbered, but if anyone could pull this off, I knew it was this man—this dragon. "Ready."

It took less than five seconds for Eliath to scale the building and land soundlessly on the third floor balcony, far enough to the side of the French doors that we were safely out of sight. I slid off his back and ensured my legs were done wobbling before I released my choke hold on the superhuman. Falling over and announcing our presence with a loud thud would not have been ideal.

I could hear a murmur of voices through the closed doors, but couldn't make out who was speaking or what was being said.

Eliath pressed himself up against the side of the building so he could peek in. After a few moments, he pulled back and pressed his mouth to my ear. "Lightning's sitting in a chair across the room. You'll have to sneak in along the panels once I've got their attention and cut his ropes. Also— oh, *fuck.* Shut *up,* you imbecile!"

I jumped at the explicative he suddenly hissed into my ear. "What?" I mouthed.

Eliath pressed up against the wall again and looked in through the glass in the door before turning back to me. "He's provoking Bright, and it's working. I've got to get in there, *now*. You, stay put until reinforcements show up," he whispered before swinging back around to the doors. Only this time, he didn't sneak. He raised a boot-clad foot and kicked in both doors with enough force to rip them both off their hinges with a resounding *crash*.

The battle had begun.

EIGHT

LIGHTNING

"Why don't you do everyone a favor and drop the toy?"

Lightning shook his head dazedly at the sound of the all-too-familiar sneer, momentarily certain the last blow to his head had given him a concussion.

"You have *got* to be kidding me!"

Bright's jarring voice made Lightning look up through the blood-matted tendrils of hair clinging to his forehead. A large, black-clad figure stood on top of the two broken balcony doors, one sword pointed at Bright's neck, the other held out against the cluster of supes closest to him. The Shade.

What. The. Hell.

"Nope, not kidding. Put the gun down, or you're going to be a head shorter." A thin line of blood trickled from Bright's neck where the very tip of The Shade's sword pressed in.

Bright dropped his signature weapon on the floor with a clonk. "I haven't got the faintest idea what you think you're going to accomplish here. One wrong move and Earthstorm is going to crush your buddy's windpipes. I do assume he's why you're here?"

"That would be correct." The Shade nodded shortly in Lightning's direction. "So you should just go right ahead and untie him for me. I might let a few of you live, if you cooperate."

Oh, for *fuck's* sake! Lightning had absolutely no idea why The Shade was here to free him, other than perhaps some misplaced kindness toward Kathryn, but he did know that it was the exact opposite of what he'd wanted. He had wished for Kathryn to be safely out of the city by now, and if The Shade was here, then she was undoubtedly still somewhere out there, way too close to what Bright was about to bring down on St. Anthony's helpless population.

"I'm sorry, you'll let a few of *us* live?" Despite the sharp weapon piercing his skin, Bright let loose a wild laugh. "What is *wrong* with you? Did this perverse little sex triangle you two got going completely fry your brain, or did Lightning's ridiculous notion of heroism actually rub off on you? There are *thirty* of us and *one* of you. Even without my lovely *toy*, you don't stand a chance.

"You know, I used to respect you. You were a ruthless killer who got what he wanted. And now look at you—I even gave you the chance to make off with your precious human, yet here you are... ready to die to stop what you should be as eager as anyone to obtain. Pathetic." With a flick of his wrist, the corrupt mayor turned on the cameras that had been set up to point at Lightning's de-masked face. "But have it your way. I guess St. Anthony will get to see two of their greatest die on camera tonight. Though I daresay, they might be cheering when they see your guts spilling out, Shade. You never were particularly popular, were you?"

To Lightning's utter surprise, The Shade actually smiled at Bright's gloating. Perhaps he really had lost the plot.

"You know, *Mayor Wilkins*, I think you're forgetting one little thing." The Shade cocked his head, his smile widening, turning more gruesome. "Lightning and I are not the only ones in this city who finds your plan to murder and enslave every citizen in St. Anthony less than ideal."

Bright scoffed. "Oh, no, you certainly weren't. But every supe who opposed me are now dead or have fled the city. And do you really think I care one whit if you call me by my human title?" He reached up and pulled off his mask, twisting so his face was directly in line with the camera. The Shade's sword followed the movement, never cutting deeper, but staying pressed against his throat. "The time for hiding is past. *We* are the new masters of the city, and *they* will learn to bow, or get slaughtered like the sheep they truly are."

"Well, it would seem the sheep might have a thing or two to say about that," The Shade said, offering a wink to the camera. "Remember why we had that unwavering codex of never organizing against the humans? Turns out, they never liked being our servants—and they've developed the means to resist in the past few thousand years."

It was then it finally dawned on Lightning what The Shade had done. He had warned the humans. The most evil villain in the city had broken one of their founding laws to save the residents of the city he had terrorized for years.

Lightning stared in shock at the man he had fought for over a decade, allowing his preternatural senses to kick in and focus on the plaza outside of the media building Bright had dragged him to. Low rumbling, the unmistakable *tha-tha-tha* of metal propellers slicing through the air and—

The whole building shook as the missile Lightning had

picked up on hit the building, sending chunks of rubble down from the ceiling.

The humans were fighting back.

The room exploded into a cacophony of noise and movement. It didn't take the gathered supes more than two seconds to catch on to what was happening, and their rage was palpable.

"You *traitor!*" Bright hissed. "You sided with the *humans* over your *brothers!*" Quicker than even The Shade could counter, he bent for his gun and rolled out of reach of the infamous twin swords. "I am going to kill you before I slaughter every last human in this city."

Somewhat to his surprise, worry knotted in Lightning's stomach as he saw Bright aim the lethal weapon at his old enemy. But there wasn't time to reflect on such puzzling emotions, not while Bright's supes poured out through the crumbling walls to take on the humans down below. He had to get free so he could help out, and The Shade was too busy with Bright to be of any use. Blue plasma exploded from Bright's terrible weapon, sang through the room, and smashed another hole in the already breaking wall, narrowly missing The Shade.

Lightning tested his bonds, but they were still too strong, even for him. The fucker had secured them skillfully. Human screams echoed from the plaza and the streets beyond, and magic of all colors lit up the dark sky. There had to be a way to get fr—

His heart skipped a beat at the sight of blonde hair disappearing behind what was left of the curtains over by the balcony. No. No. He wouldn't have. Even The Shade wouldn't be that careless. Even as he repeated the words in his head, Lightning's fight against the ropes became much more frantic. If she was truly here... Oh, powers that be, no, no, no!

"I'm sorry, my boy. It looks like it's up to me to off the city's beloved hero. I truly wish it didn't have to be this way, but what can you do? Fate plays her hand, and we have to act to her wishes."

The familiar voice momentarily jarred Lightning out of his panic. He snapped his head around and glared up at the man he had once called a mentor. Until now, he had avoided looking at Mirome, the betrayal being too much to deal with on top of everything else. The man was as flamboyantly dressed as always, with his feathered mask and deep purple, silken suit, but behind the motley costume lay a core of hard, calculating ice.

"You called yourself my father, once," Lightning spat. "How pathetic that you must claim the will of Fate to justify what you have done to me, and to The Shade. The truth is that you are a greedy coward. Using orphaned young boys to create a devoted following to sing your praises and boost your ego. You follow Bright because you are too afraid to oppose him. I am disgusted that I ever looked up to you."

Mirome smiled thinly. "You've got to get over your daddy issues, boy. I always wanted this—as does anyone who is worthy of our ancestry. *I'm* the one who brought this to Bright years ago, after I was gifted the title of Secret Keeper. I knew he was the leader we needed for this, even before he had shown the world his true potential."

Lightning shook his head as his old teacher's words sank in. *Mirome* was behind the entire, catastrophic chain of events. The cloaked figure pulling the strings behind the scenes to ensure what would be the end of the world as they knew it. Some small part of Lightning had still held out hope that Mirome had betrayed them, even tortured Kathryn so horribly, out of fear. Somehow, it would have been easier to take if he had been a coward.

"Alas, I'm afraid this is the end of our little chat," Mirome sighed. With a flick of his wrist he conjured the golden light of his magic, letting it shine from his left hand. "Bright's going to finish off your friend any moment now, and it would look best if I've finished this unpleasant task for him by the—"

Mirome's speech ended in a gurgle.

Lightning stared at the red line that had appeared across his throat, effectively cutting open his windpipe. The super-human gargled again, the magic fading from his hand. Then blood began to spurt out in thick, heavy pulses, covering Lightning's face and chest. Seconds later, Mirome fell to the floor with a *thud*. Dead.

Lightning blinked at the corpse. Then he looked back up to where Mirome had stood only seconds before.

Kathryn stared back at him, a long knife still clutched in her trembling hand.

"What are you *doing* here?" It just came out, angry tone and all. She flinched and he took a deep breath. "I'm sorry, baby—fuck. Get me loose and I'll take you somewhere safe, okay?"

She knelt by his side without a word and brought the still-bloody knife to the magic-infused knots holding his arms and legs in place. Even with what looked to be a supremely sharp blade, it took her a little while, but the second he was free he was on his feet and clutching her in his arms.

Oh, stars above. Lightning buried his face in her hair and drew in big, greedy breaths, sucking the smell of her into his lungs. She felt so soft and good against him, and he could have held her like that for an eternity, if not for the boom of Bright's latest shot being accompanied by a shout of agony. The Shade had finally failed at jumping out of range in time.

"Stay hidden!" he hissed at Kathryn as he practically shoved her down behind the anchors' desk and out of sight. "I've got to help him!"

At the other end of the studio, Bright aimed his gun at The Shade, who was crouched on the floor, clutching his stomach. Blood seeped from between his fingers.

Lightning gritted his teeth and ran. Despite his body's strained state, he crossed the short distance in the blink of an eye, coming up behind the corrupt mayor as Bright's finger tensed against the trigger.

Lightning didn't pause to think before he put both hands around Bright's neck an twisted hard. It broke between his fingers with a satisfying crack.

Bright's body slid to the floor, hand still wrapped around the infamous gun. His eyes were open and staring up at the ceiling, a look of shock permanently frozen onto his features.

"Took you long enough." The Shade wheezed. The effort made him cough, a bit of blood staining his lips in the effort.

Lightning bent and grabbed Bright's gun from his still-warm hand before giving The Shade a short look. "Are you dying?"

"Nah." Another cough. "Just need to heal a bit. Don't suppose you want to give me a hand?"

Lightning scoffed, then bent and grabbed Bright's corpse with his free hand so he could sling it up over his shoulder. "Maybe later. I'm gonna go let our Brothers and Sisters know their beloved leader's dead and see if they want to surrender. Keep Kathryn safe."

She was still huddled behind the desk, her head on her knees, and with all the fighting happening outside, Lightning deemed it safe enough to leave her behind in The Shade's care, even if he was a bit battle worn.

The streets below DNSA's crumbling building were mayhem. Humans lay dying in droves, but Lightning spotted a couple of supes among them too. It would seem The Shade had been right in his assumption that modern weaponry could present a threat to supes, even if the costs were great.

For several blocks around the plaza, St. Anthony was burning. Thick smoke billowed among the frequent flashes of offensive magic and weapon fire, and sounds of battle echoed through the streets.

Lightning sucked in a deep breath, the stench of gunpowder and singed concrete filling his lungs as he infused his body with every ounce of magic he had left. With as much power as he could possibly muster, he roared.

The sound wave was visible. It boomed across the plaza and hit the burning ruins surrounding it, shattering what little glass was still left. The humans—mainly police officers and agents—covered their ears and dropped to the ground, and every supe on the plaza and in the air above twisted around mid-fight to stare. The Call of the Dragon was impossible to ignore.

"Bright is dead," Lightning yelled once he was certain all eyes were on him. He tossed the corpse to the ground, where it landed with a visceral *splat*. "It's over. Surrender now and you may be spared. Enough blood has been spilled tonight."

NINE

KATHRYN

I've never felt such complete and utter exhaustion as I did after the battle for St. Anthony, but it was nothing compared to the relief flooding my body while I watched the aftermath, sagging between Lightning and Eliath. We had won.

Bright's body was still visible from where we were sitting on a chunk of concrete that had once been part of a major office building's wall. Someone had made a half-hearted attempt at putting police tape up around where Lightning had dropped him to the ground, but no one had gotten around to covering his corpse. They were too busy with the surprising amount of supes who had surrendered.

But our victory had come at a steep price.

Bright's corpse was far from the only body littering the plaza, and the destruction to the center of town was unlike anything the city had ever faced before. As thankful as I was that I and both the men I loved had made it through alive, it was hard to feel particularly victorious surrounded by so much death and destruction.

"How did you convince the chief to come?" Lightning

turned his head from the chaos in front of us to look at Eliath.

Eliath grimaced. "Had to reveal my identity."

Lightning's eyebrows shot up. "You sacrificed your identity to save the city?"

"To save you," Eliath sighed. He reached up and pulled off his mask. "This soulmate shit... it needs to be the three of us."

Lightning stared hard at his enemy, his eyes narrowed. "Elias Shaw. I assume you had an ulterior motive by befriending me?"

"Eliath. Might as well know my true name, since we're sharing a woman. And of course I had an ulterior motive." Eliath rubbed his shaved head and turned back to look at the police and medics rushing around. He did not deign to elaborate.

I pressed in closer to Lightning to interrupt what was bound to be some form of an argument. I just didn't have it in me to sit through the two of them bickering—not now. "Is your true name Nick? It doesn't seem all that dragon-y."

Lightning looked down at me, his eyes softening considerably. "No. It's Nicklaus."

"Nicklaus," I repeated, testing his name on my tongue. "Nicklaus."

"I could get used to the sound of you saying that." He bent to kiss the top of my head. "I want to be furious with you for putting yourself into the thick of this, but—"

"But it would be pretty ridiculous, since I saved your life?" I interrupted. I was so not in the mood to be scolded like a child.

Nicklaus grunted. "Yes. How are you doing with that? You seem better, but I know killing is hard for humans."

I shrugged. Maybe it was meant to be hard to kill, but I felt no remorse for what I'd done. Mirome was about to kill the man I loved, so I'd killed him instead. And when I thought back to what he'd done to me, a new but rather intense part of me relished the fact that I had been the one who ended his life.

Right after I'd slit his throat, though... I don't know what happened, but it had felt like my brain disconnected from my body, and a thousand images had flickered through my mind's eye while I was floating somewhere above, watching as I cut Lightning loose and then huddled behind a desk, rocking back and forth. It hadn't stopped until Eliath had teleported me down to the plaza sometime later. Perhaps the fresh air had done me good.

Though even as I thought it, I knew it wasn't the case. Something inside of me was different, somehow. Changed. Maybe Lightning was right, maybe killing Mirome was somehow messing with my mind, even if I didn't feel it yet.

"I'm okay," I said when I realized both men were staring at me with concern, as if they were afraid I could break apart into a thousand pieces any minute now. "I don't feel bad about what I did. I had to do it, and if anyone deserved it..." I trailed off, remembering that they might still be struggling with their old mentor's betrayal.

Eliath intertwined his fingers with mine, squeezing my hand. "Yes. If anyone deserved it, it was him. My only regret is that I didn't get to see his face while he struggled for his last breath."

"You were extraordinary, Kittykat," Nicklaus said. He grabbed my other hand and lifted it to his lips for a quick kiss. Then he turned his eyes back to the plaza in front of us. "Heads up"

Both Eliath and I followed his gaze and saw the Chief of Police, now covered in soot and with blood trickling from a wound on his forehead, walk toward us grimly.

I frowned and fidgeted, despite the calming warmth seeping into both my hands from my two protectors on each side. Surely, he wouldn't try to arrest Eliath along with all the other supes? Not when he was the only reason most of the city was still standing. Right?

"I see you made it through," the chief said when he stopped in front of us. "I'm not sure if that's a blessing or the opposite, but I guess it is what is is. You—" He looked at Nicklaus. "I appreciate all you've done for this city, both in your getup and as a reporter, Mr. Coleman. And I am sure there'll be some form of exception made for you, but I'd recommend leaving St. Anthony for a while. This incident won't make the general populous too keen on you supes, even the ones we owe our lives to."

His lips pinched, as if he'd sucked on a lemon as he turned his attention on Eliath. "Which brings me to you, Mr. Shaw. I realize we have you to thank for the warning of what Mayor Wilkins was planning, and I'll be sure to bring that up to the review board who'll go over your past transgressions. However, I'm afraid that, for now, you can consider yourself under arrest."

Eliath opened his mouth, undoubtedly to say something very *The Shade*-ish, but Nicklaus cut him off.

"Yeah, that's not happening, Chief." Nicklaus wiggled the gun he'd been casually pointing toward the kneeling and unmasked supes the police were busy with, ensuring they stay put. "Mr. Shaw is the *only* reason that I am not dead and the entire city isn't enslaved, and as such, he's not going to jail. In fact, he's not being charged with anything, or I will take your good advice and leave the city. Right now. And then I'm not entirely sure what you'll do with the pretty grumpy lot of supes you've got kneeling on the floor, there, but I doubt they'll want to stay around and thank you for the fight."

"That's blackmail, Coleman." The chief frowned, causing his wound to leak a fresh trickle of blood. "And, may I add, not very in tune with your hero status."

Nicklaus shrugged. "I'm fresh out of fucks to give about my *status* and all the other bullshit that's been built up about us supes over the years. Yeah, Shaw's a grade-A asshole, but ask yourself this—would a man who lived up to The Shade's reputation risk his own life to save the people in the city? I don't think so. I'm sure he's robbed a bank or two, and maybe even killed a few scumbags along the way, but in the grand scheme of things... I'd suggest you ensure he won't be prosecuted, so all this hassle he's had with rounding up these criminal elements for you won't go to waste. What do you say, Chief? Wanna make a deal?"

The chief glared at the city's hero for a long while. Then he sighed and spat at the ground next to his worn boots. "Fine, since you're leaving me no choice. I'll pull whatever strings I need to to keep the sonofabitch out of the courtroom. But be warned—the City will likely demand your valuables in return. That goes for both of you. Consider your assets seized. St. Anthony thanks you for your contribution toward its rebuild."

Eliath narrowed his eyes in obvious displeasure, but once again, Nicklaus intervened.

"Happy to do our part. And speaking of... what have you got planned for those guys?" Nicklaus nodded toward the captured supes. "I'm not planning on hanging around pointing this thing at them forever."

For the first time since I'd met him, the chief looked uncertain, as if he regretted what he was about to say. "I don't really see that we have an option. We don't have jail cells that can hold them."

The loaded silence that followed made me realize what he meant.

"You can't kill them!" I squeaked and jumped down from the block of concrete, too shocked to sit still. "They surrendered!"

"And what else do you suggest we do with them, Miss Smith? Set them free?"

"Of course not. They need to be secured in leaden cells. As long as they're completely surrounded by pure lead, they won't be able to use their... powers." My voice died down when I realized what I'd said. Where the hell did *that* come from?

"Lead?" The chief stared at me as if I'd grown two heads. "What on earth are you talking about, girl?"

"I'm... I'm not sure how I know, but I'm certain," I said, frowning as my mind's eye was assaulted by swirling masses of images, all adding pieces of information to my conscious thought process faster than I could comprehend. "Lead itself doesn't hurt them, but if they're completely surrounded by it, their powers are cut off."

Just then, I caught Nicklaus staring at me out of the corner of my eye, and turned to look at him. "I... how do I know this?"

"You killed Mirome." His voice was only just above a whisper.

"You're the new Secret Keeper." Eliath sounded as

astounded from my other side. When I whirled around to look at him, there was awe in his eyes.

"I... but... how?" I stuttered, at the same time as the Chief asked, "She's the what now?"

"She is the Secret Keeper," Nicklaus repeated. This time, his voice carried its usual assurance and authority, though his face still had a look of wonder. "She is the only living link between humans and superhumans. If you kill these supes, there is every chance that others will come to the city and seek revenge. It could easily spiral out of control and turn into a global repeat of what we've seen here tonight. How many lives would be lost?

"Maybe, if you work with Kathryn, we can find a new way to coexist. She is the only one who has a chance at bringing peace to our city."

TEN

KATHRYN

In truth, it hadn't been that long since I was in my apartment last, but as I collapsed on the couch, it felt like it had been years. Everything had changed, and the loft that had been the only place I'd ever felt safe was now like walking into a stranger's home.

Still, after everything I'd been through, it felt great to finally be able to sit down and know that my life wasn't in any immediate danger. At least, not as long as no other supe knew about my new position in their hierarchy.

"Is there any other incident of a human gaining dragon powers in that new encyclopedia you've got lodged in your pretty head?"

I shot Eliath a glare as he dropped his brown leather weekend bag next to my coffee table and fell onto the couch by my side, making me bounce from the impact. "It's not exactly like looking something up in an encyclopedia, you know. Information just pops up like it pleases, and apart from the incident with the lead... nothing's turned up so far."

"You'll need to work on that. Find a way to search

through all the knowledge, if you're going to be the Super-human Ambassador who ensures peace between our races," Nicklaus said as he flopped down next to me after parking his hardshell suitcase next to my bed, stretching both arms out along the backrest with a groan. We had made short pit stops at both supes' homes to grab a few personal items before the City Council made good on the threat to seize their assets. "Ugh, I've never been this exhausted in my entire goddamn life."

"*You* are the one who volunteered me for that job!" I snapped my head around to glare at my other superhuman lover. "You could be more helpful."

"Nah, you got this, Kittykat." Nicklaus curled an arm around my shoulders, but didn't open his eyes. From the lines on both their faces, it was obvious he wasn't joking about the exhaustion. "I've got no idea how you got all our race's history transferred when you're as human as they come, but if there's one thing I've learned from this whole, fucked up experience, it is that if anyone can use the title of Secret Keeper for good, it's you."

A swirl of images made it to the forefront of my mind. "It's the soulmate-thing. Dragon mates infuse some of their power into each other, which must be why I... Oh."

Eliath smiled lazily and reached down to squeeze my thigh before leaning his head back so he could let his eyelids flutter shut. "Yeah, you're gonna do just fine, Kitten."

We sat in silence for a while, both Nicklaus and Eliath seemingly resting, though I could tell from their breathing they weren't asleep. And I... I thought about who I was now. I knew I still looked the same, that I physically was still the same—a short and chubby girl with no particularly outstanding features. But on the *inside*... yeah, there were changes. I had been tortured and beaten and kidnapped, I had witnessed more murders than I cared to recall, and I had even killed a man myself. Yet somehow, all the violence carried the least impact when I thought about the past few weeks in the company of superhumans—in the company of dragon descendants.

All my life I had been shy and timid, and to be very honest, my self-confidence had been pretty shaky at the best of times. I had listened every time I'd been told I was nothing special, that I should never think my opinion, my voice, mattered. And yet here I was, the Secret Keeper of every Superhuman on the planet and the only person who could ensure peace among our two races, if Nicklaus was to be believed.

I think the old me would have run away and hid at such responsibility. I wouldn't have believed I had the strength or the capability to see it through, but now, I knew I could—and would. I'd survived everything Bright had thrown at me, and I had come out stronger on the other side. Nicklaus and Eliath were right—I had this. Or at least, I would, once I got the hang of how this Secret Keeper business worked.

And that was the other thing that had changed...

Nicklaus and Eliath.

Thinking back, I found it almost laughable that I'd angsted so much about what I felt for them, and how hung up I'd been on my perception of what they would and wouldn't want. It was really quite simple, in the end, because it didn't matter what any of us wanted—we belonged together. Three parts of the same unity, tied together by fate.

The images in my head whirling to explain the concept to me were not perfectly clear as to why some dragon descendants found a life partner among the humans, while most never did. Decades of speculation over generations of Secret Keepers was layered with what little knowledge there actually was, but it didn't matter. I knew in my bones I belonged with them, with both of them, and the closest word in existence to describe our connection was *soulmates*.

Sadly, that didn't mean it was all smooth sailing for us. We still knew very little about each other, and while I'd found surprising depths to both men's personalities in our short time together, I wasn't kidding myself. They were both supremely dominant and downright bossy—traits I didn't particularly care to be on the receiving end of.

And then there was their deep-seated hatred for each other.

I frowned. Surely, our connection had gone some way to heal the rift between them, seeing as they had both risked their own lives to save the other. Though, if I were to be completely honest, I wasn't entirely sure how much of that was solely for my benefit. Probably a pretty big part.

Soulmates or not, whatever the cause of their animosity, it needed to be fixed if we were going to have a shot at happiness together, and it looked like it might be my job to get them on the right path.

"So, seeing as the city has claimed all your assets, I take it you're both poor now?" My voice rung with enough sarcasm to make both of them crack an eyelid at me. "And crashing on my couch?"

Nicklaus flashed me a wry grin before he closed his eyes again. "We're dragon descendants, Kathryn. We'll never be *poor*. I've got a few offshore accounts, and I'm sure The Shade... *Eliath* has a minor business empire set up in a Third World country somewhere, with or without slave labor."

Eliath ignored the dig in favor of affording me a downright wicked smirk. "And I don't know about him, but *I* certainly won't be staying on the couch."

I rolled my eyes. "Well, then maybe it's about time we talk about where we go from here?"

Nicklaus groaned. "I take it you don't mean to bed?"

"Well, if you think you and Eliath are planning on spooning each other, go right ahead. I'd just like to know exactly what the plan is here. You both share me, until one of you snaps and kills the other?"

There was a significant silence from both men, but neither of them seemed to be resting this time. They were all furrowed brows and grimly set jaws.

"I can tell you right now that I'll never be okay with choosing between you, so don't even ask. I love you both so much, and I know I'm meant to be with both of you.

"So if you want this—if you want me—you'll have to find a way to work out your issues with each other. One thing this weird Ancient Knowledge-thing Mirome dropped on me has made very clear, is that we all need each other to get through life, especially with everything that's happened. And for that, you will need to be able to trust each other. Completely."

You could have cut the tension in the room with a knife. I was beginning to think that they were going to keep staring at each other in deadly silence forever, until Nicklaus finally broke the ice.

"You don't know what he did." It was impressive he could even manage to get the words out, with the level of strain his jaw was set with.

"No, I don't," I said, opting for as soothing a tone as I could muster. With everything we'd been through, it would be just my luck if what peace we had found was ruined because I pressured them too much. "But why don't you tell me?"

Nicklaus gave me one long, agonized look before he turned his eyes on Eliath, and his gaze hardened. "Back in the day, we were acolytes training under Mirome. He took in orphaned supe kids—Thorn and Whirl, Eliath and I—and we had all known each other from we were very young. We were friends. We were going to rule the city together, one day. Pure, youthful stupidity, of course, but Mirome encouraged it. He probably thought we'd be capable of doing what Bright eventually tried.

"In our quest for power, we did increasingly stupid shit, like challenging grown supes while dodging Mirome's and the Council's notice. No adult would ever admit to losing to a group of adolescents. We thought we were untouchable. Of course, it went wrong. It had to.

"One of the supes we'd challenged surprised us with an ambush. We were out-numbered and out-powered. And... he wasn't going to let us off with a slap on the wrist and an attitude adjustment." Nicklaus paused, his jaw working as he brought back the past events. I reached out and twined my hand with his, offering him what support I could. Though his eyes were still cold, it was obvious that the memory was very painful.

"That's when The Shade—Eliath—betrayed us. In order to save himself, he pledged his allegiance to this man and killed Whirl and Thorn to prove himself. That marked the end of our service to Mirome. And, as you can imagine, our friendship."

I was stunned.

Somewhere along the way I'd convinced myself that Eliath—that *The Shade*—wasn't as bad as the rumors would have everyone believe, and that whatever strife was between him and his archenemy could be solved somehow. But how did you ask a man to get past a betrayal like that?

"It always pissed me off how willing you were to think the very worst of me." Eliath's voice carried the unmistakable note of bitterness—of age-old resentment.

"Well, you made it real fucking easy," Nicklaus snarled, his coolness gone as if evaporated in the heat of this burning hatred between them.

"It never occurred to you that it wasn't just my own skin I saved, did it?" Eliath growled. "You're really arrogant enough to believe you made it out of that confrontation alive thanks to your own skills, aren't you?"

Nicklaus' eyes narrowed to slits. "Don't even try to—"

"To what? Tell you it was all a set-up way before we ever walked into that trap? Mirome found out about our escapades and told me he needed me to infiltrate Eruguar. He said I'd need to kill the rest of you to convince Eruguar. I argued with him, pleaded even, but you know how he was. And how we were, worshipping the ground he walked on. In the end, he told me I could let one of you live. My choice.

"I chose you—and that's the only reason you managed to escape that night."

A moment's silence passed before Nicklaus shook his head. "That's... You're lying. You're always lying to twist any situation to suit you."

"Yeah?" Eliath cocked his head as he looked at his old enemy. His old friend. "Did you never wonder why Mirome let us both out of his tutelage so easily? Did he ever try to get you back? We were fourteen—no one breaks out on their own that young. And with what we know him capable of now..."

This time, the silence stretched for several minutes. I studied Nicklaus' face as he crushed my hand in his, his every emotion playing out on his features: disbelief, denial, anger, hurt and—finally—acceptance.

"Even so," he said, "it doesn't change the fact that you killed our friends in cold blood. Without ever letting me know it was all one of Mirome's ploys. You could have ended our strife, but instead, you let it grow."

"I thought there was a reason," Eliath said. His voice was softer now, no longer hiding his vulnerability. "I trusted Mirome blindly, and he told me to never share this with a soul. At first, I thought you'd figure it out on your own, but when it became clear you wouldn't... I grew to resent you. You were my closest friend, and you never even..."

He shook his head. "I thought Mirome had some grand scheme behind keeping it a secret, but maybe he just didn't want us to join forces as adults. As for killing the others... I didn't see much of a choice. If I had refused him, he would have found me weak and chosen another to do his bidding. And you and I would have been sacrificed instead. I'm not ashamed of my choice. I never was."

My heart ached after Eliath finished his tale. They had both been so young, and in the hands of a ruthless man who had used and abused them for his own ploys. Mindlessly, I grasped after Eliath with my free hand without taking my eyes off Nicklaus. His palm closed around mine, big and strong and comforting, but I knew that this time, he was the one in need of my strength, not the other way around.

Nicklaus shook his head and his throat worked as if any words he attempted to produce got stuck. Finally, he stood up and released my hand with a small squeeze.

"Don't go." For a moment I thought he was about to leave

me again, and tears welled up in my eyes before I could stop them.

A pained spasm crossed his face, and he bent to bury both his hands in my hair so he could force my eyes to his. "No, Kathryn, no. I'm not... I'll never leave you again. I promise. I just need... a moment. Go to bed, my love. We all need to rest. I will join you shortly."

When sunlight filtered in through the windows and danced across my face, finally pulling me from a deep, dreamless sleep, Nicklaus was not in my bed.

My heart leapt into my throat for three long seconds while my mind immediately jumped to the worst possible conclusion—that he had broken his word and left me. But when I twisted my head around to scan my living room, I saw the back of him as he sat on my couch, leaned forward with his head in his hands.

Relief flowed through my system, and I sank back down into the bed for a few moments as I regained my bearings.

Eliath was still sound asleep next to me, curled around my body as if he was protecting me from the world even in his dreams. I reached out and let a finger follow his strong brow and watched as the sun danced along his handsome face. How lonely he must have been, all alone and undercover with an enemy at the age of fourteen. No matter how strong superhumans were, no one would convince me that they weren't still children at that age, and he had had to do horrible things just to stay alive. Including betraying his best friend.

I kissed him on the mouth and extracted myself without waking him. They both needed help healing their old scars, and I would do anything in my power to give it to them.

Nicklaus didn't look up when I pattered toward him on bare feet, but he did wrap an arm around me when I sat down by his side and placed a gentle hand on his back.

"Have you slept at all?"

"No." His voice was hoarse with strain and exhaustion, and more than confirmed his statement. "Too many thoughts."

I stroked his face with a gentle hand until he looked up at me. There was so much pain in his glowing eyes that it made my heart clench.

"Do you believe what Eliath told us last night?"

Nicklaus scrubbed his free hand across his face. "Yes, but that doesn't change decades of emotions in one, easy swoop. We have fought for so long, and there's been so much extra shit over the years... I know Mirome was rotten to the core now, but it's still hard to fully comprehend how profoundly he lied to us. He was the next best thing to a father to me—he took me in when I was just six years old."

"It sounds like he was something similar to Eliath," I said.

"Yeah." Nicklaus sighed and held me closer, wrapping his other arm around my t-shirt clad body. I hadn't been able to bring myself to get into my trusty footie pajamas the night before, not with the two supes around. "I'm going to try, Kathryn. I know he's your soulmate as much as I am, but it might take some time. It doesn't matter, though. Being with you—it's worth everything to me."

The pure love in his eyes made a lump form in my throat. "Thank you," I whispered.

Nicklaus kissed me in response. It was soft at first, a simple meeting of our lips to confirm the emotion I had just seen in his eyes. True to form, though, that didn't last long. My head was still swimming when he deepened the kiss, delving his tongue in between my lips to taste and tease.

I groaned in response and opened for him, my needy body already clamoring excitedly for what it knew would follow. We might have had a rocky start to this somewhat unorthodox relationship, but at least the sex was one thing that had worked straight from the beginning.

Nicklaus grabbed me by the hips and lifted me up until I was kneeling on the couch with a leg on each side of his thighs, and then slid his big hands down to my ass underneath my panties. My skin felt on fire everywhere he touched me, and when he broke our kiss to start working on my neck and jawline, the burning crackle of sensation went straight to my clit.

As if he could sense it, Nicklaus moved from my behind to the front of my panties and pressed a thumb against my clit, letting the fabric crease in my folds. It wasn't until then I realized I was already wet with anticipation.

"I need to be inside of you," he rumbled against my throat. "Let me be inside of you."

"Uh-huh," I groaned in response, because he was rubbing circles against my taut clit with his thumb, ruining my ability to think about anything but the pleasure of being with him—even the fact that Eliath was still asleep on the bed behind us.

His grip on me strengthened as he stood up. I wrapped my legs around his hips and my arms around his neck, allowing a tiny thrill at being lifted and carried so easily to seep through my mounting desire. As short as I was, I'd always been too heavy for most men to lift me with ease. The contrast between Nicklaus and Eliath treating me like a fragile little thing most of the time, while fully capable of throwing me around the bedroom with all the strength of their dragon ancestry in the heat of passion, was very appealing after a lifetime of feeling like I was never quite feminine enough.

"I am only complete when you are wrapped around me," Nicklaus whispered hotly into my ear before he captured the lobe between his teeth, sending shivers of raw anticipation down my spine. Then he released my grip on his body and threw me down. My back hit the bed and made it bounce, but I didn't have time to protest the treatment before Nicklaus was on top of me, completely naked. Super speed really did have its advantages.

I stared up into his glowing eyes, lost in their overwhelming need—a need that resonated deep within my own soul. Then I felt a sharp tug around my waist accompanied by the ripping sound of fabric being torn in half. Nicklaus gave me a wicked smile and dipped down, disappearing from my immediate field of vision.

"*Oh!*" His tongue stroked up between my lower lips, spreading my slit from bottom to top in one, easy lick that ended in a few teasing swipes over my clit. Then he delved back down again, sucking and tasting my inner folds while completely ignoring my nub of increasingly hyperaware nerves.

I reached for his blond hair to force his head up where I wanted it most, but before I even got to touch his soft locks, my hands were grabbed and roughly yanked up over my head.

"Hey!" I struggled against the tight grip around my wrists, but to no avail. All it did was make Nicklaus place both hands on my inner thighs so he could keep my lower body still for his continued exploration. "What—?"

Eliath's sleepy face popped into view, one eyebrow raised in challenge. "Yes?" He wasn't even straining to keep me still, despite my best efforts at pulling free.

"What... what are you doing?" The surprise of suddenly being pinned by an extra set of hands cut through my arousal enough to allow uncertainty to seep through. I hadn't had much time to think about this particular aspect of our unconditional relationship, but I'd pretty much assumed that the time they both shared me was a one-off, spur-of-the-moment thing. In hindsight, I should definitely have given it some more thought, especially before I let Nicklaus toss me down on the same bed Eliath was sleeping in. Damn those pheromones and their ability to completely destroy any and all rational thought!

Eliath slanted a smile at me, the devious gleam in his eyes making my stomach flutter with just a twinge of unease. "I'm watching. For now."

Just then, Nicklaus flicked his tongue up to lap at my clit once more. I whimpered and every muscle in my body tensed, my pelvis pressing up against his mouth of its own accord to get more.

Nicklaus relented and closed his mouth around my tight bud.

I moaned with relief when he sucked the small nub into his mouth. My back arched, and my body finally began the delicious climb toward release. As always, it felt like my entire being was attuned to the man between my legs, as if I was made for every lap of his tongue and every suckle of his lips. It didn't take long before I was teetering on the edge, ready to fall.

But before I could, Nicklaus released my throbbing clit and, before I could do anything but moan in protest, lined himself up against my opened entrance and pushed in. Hard.

"*Nn-oh!*" The sensation of being taken, roughly and without warning, flowered up through my body from my achingly full pussy in one long, fitful spasm. I pulled against Eliath's grip on my arms to get my hands free so I could press against Nicklaus' taut stomach, try to control the invasion of my defenseless channel. He didn't budge and only gave me a taunting "*ah, ah,*" as if I was a misbehaving child.

If Nicklaus noticed Eliath's interference, he didn't mind. When he drew back only to slam in hard again the next second, moaning with pleasure, I thought that maybe he even liked seeing me helplessly held down for him. Forced to take all his pent-up anguish and desire.

It hurt a little, as it always did when I first took either of them inside of me, but it was drowned out by the rush of endorphins and pure, sharp bliss.

I let my head fall back down to the mattress as Nicklaus began fucking me in earnest, hard, deep and fast, though he spared me his preternatural speed. Perhaps it was my love for them both, or the trust I had in the fact that they would never, ever hurt me, but the element of force triggered every ounce of fervor and lust in my body. Being truly *taken,* overwhelmed and consumed with this man's, this superhuman's, desire for me—it brought out every debauched desire and fantasy I'd ever had before meeting my soulmates.

I spread my legs wider and gasped with every ruthless thrust, letting him know I felt his strength and need with every fiber of my being. That I wanted it, all of it.

Soon, I was climbing the heights of ecstasy once again.

Though my clit wasn't being stimulated, Nicklaus was so thick that every sensitive part of my pussy was being rubbed and pleasured intensely. I had never been able to come just from penetration before the two of them, but then again, I was fairly sure no human man had a cock this big. Or knew how to fuck me just right. Nicklaus' pace quickened as if he felt the spasms in my desperately clenching pussy and knew what they meant.

"Come with me, Kathryn," Nicklaus panted as he pounded me. "I want you to come on my cock as I spill my seed in you."

I drew in a breath, so close to the point of no return I could practically feel it, but something held me back from tumbling over. I clenched my hands uselessly above my head, straining against Eliath's grip to find purchase for that last push over the edge.

Eliath tightened his hold on me, as if he was steeling me against my own body's violent tremors. "Give in, baby. Come for us, Kitten—let go."

Deep shivers traveled down through my arms from where he held me, and then up again from my abdomen in sharp, short bursts until the dam broke and I came, hard.

"*Yes, yes yes!*" I don't know who among us gasped those words out like a mantra while my body seized, my pussy clutching tightly at Nicklaus' pulsing cock. My world was a torrent of pleasure that made my eyes roll back and my hips rise and fall in fitful waves as if to draw every last drop of my lover's release deep into my womb.

When my orgasm finally ebbed, allowing me to collapse again, Nicklaus followed. His sides surged with his fast pants for breath as he rested on top of me, forehead pressed against mine.

Eliath released my wrists with a gentle stroke, but I grasped for him again with one hand, wanting to feel him while I came down from my high. The other I lifted to Nicklaus' back so I could stroke him while he calmed down. His eyes were still closed when I looked at him, but his mouth curved in a soft smile at my caress. "You okay?"

"Mmhm," I purred and stretched happily out underneath him. His cock was still semi-hard inside of me, and the friction from my movement made a small tremor shoot up from where we were connected. Seemed like my pussy was starting to warm up to the idea of servicing two men. "And you?"

He opened his eyes then, bathing me in the blue glow of his preternatural gaze. "Much better." Then he sighed and straightened up, looking straight at Eliath. "Your turn."

Eliath tutted and tickled my arm. "Come now, Nicklaus. Do you only have one go in you? Don't you want to stay inside her blessed little pussy for another round?"

Nicklaus arched both eyebrows. "It's quite evident you're bursting to take over, so what game are you playing here? I'm too tired to deal with your shit."

"No game. See it as my attempt at an olive branch—I just want to watch the two of you together, for now."

Eliath was most assuredly playing some sort of game, but I had no idea what he was hoping to win at the end of it. But apparently, either Nicklaus actually believed him, or he didn't care, because he just grunted and fell back down on top of me. This time, though, he caught himself in both arms, and instead of resting, he rocked his hips against mine.

I gasped sharply, all thoughts of Eliath's scheming dispersing as the thick cock inside of me began to grow. My pussy, still wet from before and now also soaked with Nicklaus' cum, adjusted to accommodate him without pain this time. I moaned as he took me with slow, measured thrusts. My lust rose lazily up through my abdomen, pushing away the lethargic aftermath of my prior orgasm for every time he bottomed out in my tight sheath.

"Ride him, Kitten," Eliath whispered in my ear. "He will love it as much as I did."

I didn't pause to think why Eliath was giving me instructions on how to best please the man he had claimed to hate up until last night. In hindsight, I undoubtedly should have, but in that moment it just sounded like a sexy idea. I wanted Nicklaus to feel every ounce of my passion as I speared myself on his deliciously thick cock, and to watch his eyes burn with passion as he struggled to remain passive underneath me, just like Eliath had.

I reached up to push at Nicklaus' shoulder. He protested with a rumbling grunt when I rolled him off me and he slipped out of my body, but when I climbed on top of him and spread my knees so I could straddle his hips, he relaxed and let me shove him the rest of his way onto his back.

Despite the eager erection pressing up hard against my ass and the lust evident in his eyes, I could see lines of exhaustion on his face now that the light from the windows shone directly on it.

"Just let me take care of you," I murmured. I reached out to stroke his face, and his eyelids fluttered shut at the contact. Once again I was overwhelmed with the magnitude of what he had done for me. He had offered up his own life and undoubtedly suffered through torture and humiliation in Bright's hands, all so I could live. "It's my turn to give you everything now."

With that, I raised up just high enough to capture his straining cock against my nether lips. I braced myself with one hand on his chest and grabbed his pulsing length with the other so I could guide it in. His blunt head spread my entrance wide and then slid home, straining against my trembling walls as I sank all the way down.

We gasped together when he bottomed out. Nicklaus' eyes popped open again, and I was rewarded with exactly the kind of burning passion I'd hoped for.

I offered him a cheeky smile, and then I moved.

Nicklaus groaned and grabbed for my knees. For a moment I thought he'd take over again, but he restrained himself, clutching at me as if he was holding on for dear life.

It was so unbelievably empowering to see this strong, all-male superhuman struggle for self-control underneath me. I rolled my hips again, taking him all the way in, and felt his fingers dig deep into my flesh.

Determined to keep control, I leaned forward so I could support both hands on his chiseled chest while pressing him down, and then began to fuck myself on his cock with hard, fluid motions.

Nicklaus moaned softly underneath me every time I took him to the hilt, as lost in the pleasure of being together as I was. There was nothing but ecstasy and his body underneath, and inside of me. That is, until Eliath decided he was done watching.

Warm fingers skimmed up my spine, from my tailbone to my shoulder blades, raising goosebumps along my sweat-covered skin. Then they slid around to my front and were joined by their counterparts as Eliath grabbed both my breasts from behind and lifted them up, tweaking the nipples a little harder than what I liked. When I groaned in protest, he bit down on the place my shoulder met my neck, digging his strong teeth into my skin in warning.

I whimpered and went lax, my movements on Nicklaus' hard length coming to a halt. Both his teeth and his fingers, which were now rolling my nipples and tugging on them, hurt, but it was the good kind of pain—the kind that made the pleasure of being filled to the brim with Nicklaus' thick cock all the more pleasurable.

Somewhere behind the fog of endorphins, I was surprised Nicklaus didn't protest the interruption, but he just watched us, keeping his hands locked around my knees.

"You have no idea how sexy you look, sliding up and down on his dick like that, Kitten," Eliath whispered in my ear once my surrender was evident. His breath tickled my skin and raised more goosebumps down my neck. "Your little pussy having to stretch so wide every time you sit down, and the sounds it makes... I wonder if you're wet enough for more?"

I groaned unintelligibly and my pussy flexed greedily against Nicklaus' hard cock at the thought of *"more,"* whatever he meant by that. When he released my breasts and pressed me down flat onto Nicklaus' chest with a hand on my upper back, I followed willingly. Nicklaus released my knees and wrapped both his strong arms around me, pulling me as close as I could come. His cock remained hard and pulsing deep inside of me, and the new angle made it press up against my cervix. Normally, I would have flinched at that, but I was so wet and turned on it just felt good.

Eliath grabbed my ass in both hands and spread my cheeks. I felt the bed dip behind me as he moved in closer, and had a moment of concern that he might want to do anal. I'd seen enough porn to know how most threesomes ended up, and I'd never seen the appeal in having a cock forced in *there*—especially not one of Eliath's size.

But rather than focus on my backside, Eliath slipped his fingers forward until they reached my already stuffed pussy. "So wet," he murmured hoarsely. "You're soaking, Kitten. I think you need some more cock in that pretty little snatch of yours."

"Yes. Please," I groaned, more than a little relieved he wasn't planning on doing anything crazy with my poor, human body. Last time they had shared me had been the best sex of my life, and I was very ready for my lovers to take turns again. I rolled my hips a little against Nicklaus to display my eagerness to continue. "I need more, now."

"Your wish, my command," Eliath said, and it wasn't until then I caught on to the considerable wickedness in his lust-roughened voice. But before I could think more about it, he'd placed a hand on my hips so I couldn't move my lower body, and with the other hand spread my already stretched outer labia wide enough to slip a finger up inside of me, next to Nicklaus' cock.

Nicklaus grunted, and I gasped in shock at the sudden extra tension. My pussy had only started to get accustomed to the size of superhuman cock very recently, and Eliath didn't have slender fingers.

Nicklaus raised an eyebrow at him above my shoulder, but he didn't object to Eliath's rather intimate proximity to his private parts. And when the villain forced another finger into my pussy, and I tried to rear up from the intense stretch,

Nicklaus tightened his grip around me so I couldn't get up, capturing my lips with his.

I whimpered into his mouth, and he responded with scorching heat. He held me there, trapped by his kiss until my pussy managed to adjust to Eliath's fingers.

When I finally could relax against his torso, Nicklaus pulled his head back and breathed deeply with me. "Fuck, that's so tight."

"Help me get her ready." Eliath's voice was dark and deep with pent-up desire. I felt him twist his fingers gently inside of me, and tensed up again at the pressure.

"W-what are you do—*oh!*" I ended my question with a whimper, because Nicklaus started to move with Eliath's twisting, thrusting gently up into me. He couldn't have been moving more than an inch or two, but because I was forced open so wide, it felt like every single part of my pussy was being stimulated far beyond anything I'd ever experienced before.

"Look at me, baby," Nicklaus groaned underneath me. "Look into my eyes."

I obeyed, though it was hard to focus on him as long as they were both moving in alternating patterns, driving me crazy with stimulation I wasn't sure I could handle.

"We would never hurt you, you know that, right?" Nicklaus asked. His arms around my upper torso squeezed me gently as if to reassure my trembling form.

"Yes," I gasped. I knew that, even if they were both doing things to my body I wasn't sure I could withstand. These men would never, ever harm me.

"Good girl," he whispered and captured my mouth for another kiss, lighter this time and much shorter. "Then relax for us, my love. Everything is all right. Relax and enjoy it. You know we got you."

I did know that. I breathed deeply and closed my eyes again, willing my body to follow his command.

The sensations inside of me changed the moment I did. From being too much to bear it was suddenly just right, and my whimpers quickly became fueled by my need for more, rather than discomfort or fear.

"Such a good girl," Eliath growled from behind me as he kept up the gently twisting pattern against my quivering walls. "Fuck, you're gushing, you're so wet."

"Make me come," I pleaded mindlessly. The tension inside of me was racking up my abdomen and setting every nerve ending in my body on fire. I needed release from the exquisite torture, or I feared I would burn alive from the smoldering heat they stoked deep inside of me. "Please, you have to make me come."

"Happy to," Eliath said, but instead of reaching for my clit, he slipped both fingers out of my swollen pussy while Nicklaus stilled his gentle thrusts. But before I could voice my frantic disapproval, I felt Eliath's hands slid up my back to my shoulders as the bed shifted with his weight.

I whimpered impatiently and flexed my hips as much as I could with Nicklaus still lodged all the way inside, trying to tempt Eliath back to my weeping entrance.

Soon, his hands returned to my ass, opening me up to his inspection again, and I groaned with relief. Then something blunt and wide and much, much bigger than a finger pressed up against my already full pussy, seeking entrance. His rock hard cock.

My heart skipped a beat when I finally realized what he was trying to do. "No, no, you can't, it won't fit! Are you crazy?" I wailed in the beginning stages of panic. I tried to sit back up, but Nicklaus held me down with his unyielding grasp around my upper body.

"Shh, relax, my love," he said, his tone gentle even though his blue eyes were dark with lust. "Trust us. You're safe, I promise. Relax and let it happen. It needs to happen."

I had absolutely no idea why "*it needed to happen,*" but I did trust them, and just being reminded of that calmed me down a little. I stared into Nicklaus' eyes as he continued to talk soothingly at me, while Eliath pressed gently against my splayed lips. It felt like he was testing my body's resistance rather than trying to force his way in, and between Nicklaus' soft coaxing and Eliath's gentle pressure, I finally relaxed fully.

Eliath grunted when my body finally went lax, and I felt the tip of his finger slip in above Nicklaus' cock like a wedge, but before I could tense a single muscle in response, his finger was replaced by something much thicker.

I had never thought my body could open so wide. I cried out in shock of the brutal stretch when his fat mushroom head pressed in alongside Nicklaus, and then again when Eliath slowly slid the full length of his cock all the way up inside my defenseless pussy.

"*Fuck!* Oh, fuck, fuck, *fuck!*"

I had no idea which of them swore at the sensation of being clenched together by my spasming pussy, and I was only faintly aware of Nicklaus going rigid beneath me as Eliath froze on top of me, his fingers digging into my hips as if in cramps, because all I could think of and all I could sense was the brutal stretch.

It hurt.

I was dimly aware that there was pain, from my savagely

stretched opening and all the way up to where their blunt cock heads forced my inner most channel as wide as it would go, but it was as if my mind couldn't quite comprehend it. As if the pain was drowned out by the flood of endorphins being pumped through my blood with every pulse of my frantically beating heart.

My vision swam, leaving me blinded, and even the sounds of my lovers' harsh gasps for air and growled curses as they themselves adjusted to the new sensations died down to a muted throbbing in tune to my pulse.

Slowly, my body began to adjust, and as it did, I was bombarded with every sensory impression forced into me by the two thick cocks in my pussy.

It was a strange mix of purely physical sensations, like the raw, feminine pleasure of being utterly filled to the brim, and the pain that seemed to mix with the ecstasy to a delicious, agonizing blend, but also emotions I hadn't expected. There was a deep, primal satisfaction of being taken so completely, of giving over my body to two males, trust so overpowering it seemed to fill every cell in my body, and the knowledge that I was loved and cared for more deeply than I had ever thought possible. I wanted to scream, to laugh, to cry.

When they began to move, I think I did all three.

They were slow at first, and very gentle, but to my over-stuffed pussy, it felt like I was being pummeled. They moved in alternating patterns, one sliding halfway out while the other pushed in deeper, tormenting my G-spot and every sensitive part of my tender tissue along with it. The first orgasm was near-instant.

"Good girl," Eliath groaned from behind me as I

thrashed helplessly between them, speared on their double intrusion as I was. *"Fuck, that's—ugh!"*

I knew why he was moaning, and Nicklaus along with him, because my pussy was clamping down hard on both of them in a useless attempt to expel them from my depths while I rode through my orgasm. When my climax finally passed and I collapsed back down on Nicklaus' chest, we were all panting for air.

"Holy fuck, woman," Nicklaus growled after a few moments of catching his breath. "Are you trying to kill us?"

"Kill *you?*" I gasped, and moaned when my pussy flexed experimentally around them. I would have said something more, but the sensation that involuntary spasm sent through my system erased all words from my brain. Evidently, my orgasm had allowed my pussy to adjust to the vast gape, letting me feel nothing but the most intense pleasure of my life.

As if they read my body perfectly, both men began to move again at my prolonged moan, and this time, they weren't nearly as gentle. They fucked me with long, full thrusts, never breaking their seesawing rhythm, and I went wild between them.

I came, screaming like a banshee, but this time, they didn't stop—only pounded me through my orgasm, prolonging it until my throat was hoarse and my pussy couldn't contract any more, and then they fucked me harder and faster. I came again, and their cocks never stopped forcing their way up my trembling pussy, pumping me mercilessly over and over and over.

Time stopped making sense, and I lost count of how many times I came for them, but by the end of it I was sobbing through every one. Every orgasm hurt, I was that oversensitive, and my muscles were like jelly from the violent contractions that wracked my body every few minutes. And yet it was the most exquisite form of torture, and I never wanted it to end.

When it finally did, I was moments from passing out. My vision had gone black, and the roar of first Eliath and then Nicklaus were muted, but I felt the rush of their seed bathing my cervix in a warm flood. They both stilled, only gently rocking back and forth within me for a few moments, teasing my body to prolong the final tremors of my latest orgasm for a few excruciating seconds.

Eliath collapsed down on top of me, his large form pressing me into Nicklaus' chest. I moaned in a weak protest of his weight, and he shifted just enough that I could breathe unhindered again.

"Well, that was... something else," Nicklaus said after several minutes of complete silence, with the only sound in the loft being our ragged breathing.

"Mmhm," Eliath agreed, without as much as looking up from where his head was cradled against my neck. "You doing okay, Kitten?"

"No," I rasped. My throat was dry after all the screaming, and strands of hair stuck to my sweaty face and made my skin itch, but I was too boneless to do anything about it. "You killed me. I'm pretty sure you straight-up murdered me, and I'm actually dead right now."

Nicklaus made an amused sound in his throat and planted a light kiss on my lips. "Perhaps we best pull out then, hm? Necrophilia never was my thing."

"You're such a funny guy," I mumbled. If I'd had more energy, I'm sure it would have succeeded in coming off as sarcastic as I'd meant it.

"He's got his moments." Eliath sounded way more amused than I was. He planted a kiss at the top of my spine and then gently raised up so he could slide out of my swollen opening.

I winced, and scrunched up my face at the sensation of semen flooding out of me when first he, and then Nicklaus, pulled out of my sore body.

Nicklaus rolled me gently off his chest so I was sprawled out in my best imitation of a starfish on the bed next to him. Eliath collapsed on my other side with a deep groan.

Silence spread once more as we all fell back into quiet contemplation of what had just happened. Or, that was what I assumed we were all doing, up until I realized Nicklaus was snoring faintly.

The outrage gave me enough strength to slap an arm across his chest, startling him back awake. "Oi!"

"You realize I haven't slept in over twenty-four hours, right?" he grumbled.

I gave him a reproachful glare before closing my eyes again. "You can sleep *after* you two explain to me what the hell just happened."

"We fucked," Eliath said with a content sigh. "A lot." Helpful, as always.

"Yes, thank you, I got that part. What I'm slightly more fuzzy on is why you two decided to, ah..." My mind did its best to come up with a delicate description of what we'd just done, but failed miserably. "Cross swords."

Nicklaus gave a grunt of laughter and rested an arm across his eyes, shielding them from the light. The other he scooped under my neck so I could rest in the crook of his elbow. "I think you should take this one, *Shade*."

Eliath rolled over halfway so he was resting on his side. I

could feel his eyes on my face, but didn't have the energy to open mine and return his gaze. "It was a magic-thing. Or a mark-thing, if you will. We both claimed you, but we've been fighting each other for you all along. When our semen mixed inside of you, so did our magic—our essence. It's something we needed to do to help settle our anger and frustration with each other."

"Really?" I managed to crack an eyelid at him. "All you needed to do was mix sperm, and now you no longer hate each other?"

"Well, it's not quite that simple." The corner of his mouth twitched at my crude explanation. "We still have our history, but being that intimate... it's surprisingly healing."

"Mmhm," Nicklaus agreed from underneath the shelter of his arm. "Just a few dozen rounds of double vaginal to go and we're sure to become BFFs. Hopefully, we didn't kill you so bad you won't want to do it again once you've had a bit of a break. You know, for our relationship's sake."

I blinked. Repeatedly. "He's joking, right?" I asked Eliath, whose smile had grown exponentially at Nicklaus' words.

"Eh, I doubt we'll ever paint teach other's toenails or anything, even if you do have quite the magical cunt, but I'm sure it wouldn't be a bad idea if we revisited this 'sword crossing' thing a few times a month."

I was fairly sure they were both screwing with me, but the sight of Eliath's teasing smirk made me give up arguing and close my eyes again. I was way too tired to make any sort of headway with either stubborn male, and besides—despite my nether region's weak protests at the idea—I was pretty sure I wouldn't mind "revisiting" the morning's playtime once I'd had some time to rest.

Yawning, I reached out a hand to grab Eliath by the wrist, pulling him with me as I twisted against Nicklaus' warm body. Eliath came willingly and shielded my body with his, curling up behind me so I was once again completely sandwiched between my two lovers.

Who knew, maybe they were telling the truth—maybe being together like this would actually help heal their relationship, and if that's the case I was certainly a willing participant. There wasn't anything in this world I wouldn't do for either of them. Especially not if it came with as many orgasms as this one had.

"I love you," I mumbled, already halfway drifting off into the arms of sleep. "So much."

"We love you too, Kathryn. Always and forever."

"I still don't understand how you two did this to me. I was on the pill, for Chrissake!"

Nicklaus slid both arms around me from behind and rested his hands on my swollen belly, peering at us in the mirror over my shoulder. We were both dressed to the nines, and despite my gloomy mood, I couldn't help but appreciate how handsome he was in his designer suit.

"It kind of comes with the territory of being a supe, I suppose," he said and placed a kiss on the side of my neck in that way that always caused shivers to travel down the length of my spine. I frowned at him in the mirror for his obvious attempt at distracting me. "Superhumans have super sperm —it makes sense, doesn't it?"

"That's not how birth control works," I growled. "Look at me! I can barely get off the couch on my own these days! Not to mention stay awake for more than three hours at a time. How am I meant to make the President consider implementing any sort of pro-supe changes to the Superhuman Bill when all I can think about is having another nap?"

An amused chuckle warned of Eliath's arrival in the dressing room in the well-concealed apartment my two betrothed had bought for us. He slid in front of the mirror, blocking off my view of my own, round shape and embracing me gently so I was sandwiched between the two of them. "You'll do fine, Kitten. We'll dance and be seen by all the media, and then you'll have a casual chat with him in view of everyone. The world knows what's at stake if the supes take offense to the legislation, my love, and they know you're our ambassador. He will listen."

I frowned and pressed my face into his expensive shirt. Being held like this, between the two of them, always calmed me down—at least some. Especially now that any lingering animosity between them had died with the revelation of my pregnancy shortly after the battle for St. Anthony. I had no proof, but I was pretty sure my bulging belly was a result of the first time they shared my body. Even first-class birth control might have to cave at the onslaught of a double dose of superhuman seed. "You make it sound like it's a walk in the park. Do you have any idea how draining the two little monsters you planted in my uterus are?"

Both men laughed, though they quickly quieted down when I gave them each an elbow to the stomach.

"Yeah, we know. The fact that you keep falling asleep mid-sex is a bit of a giveaway," Eliath said with a smirk. Nicklaus grasped my arms and held them to my body before I could use my elbows again.

"I'd like to see you juggle being ambassador-slash-Secret Keeper for a bunch of bloodthirsty dragon descendants, while being pregnant with not one, but *two* of your little devil spawn! I bet you'd need a bit of rest from the sex-marathon that is my life every once in a while, too."

Nicklaus kissed the back of my neck gently, sending another tendril of excitement down my spine. "We know, baby. You've been working non-stop since the battle for St. Anthony, and we don't give you much rest when we're alone, either. If you need a break, then you'll get one."

"I don't think there's such a thing as maternity leave in my job," I muttered. They were both stroking my body now —not to arouse, but to soothe. It worked, as it always did, and I relaxed between them.

"Perhaps not, but if you need it... we can take a break from the sex." Eliath sounded almost pained as he said it, but it still made me jerk my head back up with renewed anger.

"Don't you dare even say that! You know how horny this pregnancy makes me."

Nicklaus grunted behind me with suppressed laughter. "Yeah... yeah, we do. But you know we'll do anything for you, Kittykat, and if you need rest..."

"No," I said, aware that my tone was still on the grumpy side. "I'll get through it. The little cretins can't stay in my womb forever, anyway." A cold shock went through me the second after the words were out of my mouth. "Oh, God, they can't, can they? How long are superhuman pregnancies?" I searched frantically through the onslaught of images I pulled from the place in my mind reserved for Dragon Secrets, only to draw a relieved sigh when the right one popped to the forefront.

"Just nine months," Nicklaus said, his hands slipping back to my belly.

Eliath shifted his grip so he too could encase my round stomach in his hands. "Are you happy, Kathryn?"

I frowned again at the question. "You know I am. Why would you even ask that?"

"With them?" Nicklaus said, his thumbs grazing my silk dress just above my navel. "Our babies?"

"You've been through so much, and everything's happened very fast," Eliath rumbled. "We never talked about this, before they were here."

There was unmistakable worry in both men's voices.

I swallowed the suddenly forming lump in my throat and blinked until the pesky tears in my eyes dispersed. Damn hormones were completely out of control these days. Carefully, I placed a hand on top of theirs. The little ones within seemed to sense our combined attention and pressed back, making my belly bubble with their movements.

"I never thought I would have this," I said, my voice breaking. I cleared my throat and swallowed again, ensuring I could continue without breaking into a weeping mess of emotions. I knew from experience that that didn't exactly help reassure my lovers. "Love so strong it almost hurts to think about, a purpose that goes beyond myself, and so much joy I can hardly contain it. You've given that to me, both of you. You've put your past behind you to give this life to me, painful as it was. And you have given me these two little terrors. Two manifestations of our love for each other. Two little souls. Yes, it happened very fast, and yes, it's a lot to deal with right now, but I..."

I breathed deeply to control my swirling emotions that threatened to well up and consume me, as they so often did when I thought about my new little family.

"Yes, I am happy with them. They are the reason I work so hard, because I want them to grow up in a world where they are safe and protected. Just like you have both protected me since the day we met."

Soft lips kissed my forehead and the back of my neck,

traveled down my face to my lips and from my neck to my shoulder, showering me with affection.

The world might still be a dark and dangerous place, but with the help of my lovers—the fathers of my children—I would fight to change that.

Yes, I was happy.

He saved me... And then he blood-bonded me. Now
I'm his.

My first meeting with a Chicago vampire went better than
expected.

Up until that night, all I knew about vampires was limited to a few
common facts: they drink blood, they get a mean sunburn and if
you find yourself alone with one, you're dead.

Except he didn't kill me.

Sexy, broody Warin clearly had his own reasons for sparing my
life and tying me with his blood, but if he'd known how much

trouble I'd attract, I bet he wouldn't have bothered. When he blood-bonded me, secrets even I didn't know about myself came to light.

Secrets that will pull us both deep into the eternal war between vampires and the witches determined to rid the world of their evil.

We have only one choice now: fight the forces hell-bent on breaking our bond...

Or die.

ALSO BY NORA ASH

THE OMEGA PROPHECY

Ragnarök Rising

Weaving Fate

Betraying Destiny

DEMON'S MARK

Branded

Demon's Mark

Prince of Demons

ALPHA TIES

Alpha

Feral

ANCIENT BLOOD

Origin

Wicked Soul

Debt of Bones*

DARKNESS

Into the Darkness

Hidden in Darkness

Shades of Darkness

Fires in the Darkness

MADE & BROKEN

Dangerous

Monster

Trouble